P

At

Redhook

By

Stephen Euin Cobb

Plague at Redhook

Copyright © 1999 by Stephen Euin Cobb

All rights reserved. No part of this book may be reproduced in any form or by any electronic or mechanical means including information storage and retrieval systems, without permission in writing from the author or publisher, except by a reviewer who may quote brief passages in a review or article.

Published by: August Press
P.O. Box 5998
Aiken SC 29804-5998

ISBN: 0-9670346-1-2

Email:
victor@plagueatredhook.com

Website:
http://plagueatredhook.com

Printed in the USA by

MORRIS PUBLISHING
3212 East Highway 30 • Kearney, NE 68847 • 1-800-650-7888

This book is dedicated to my best friend. Without whose help, encouragement, suggestions, and plain hard work, this novel might never have seen the light of day. I feel doubly blessed, in that my best friend is also my wife. Thank you, Michelle. I love you.

Chapter 1

Wreckage

A man in his late-thirties with jet black hair scrambled through the spotless but unfamiliar corridors of his new ship as he watched the twisted remains of a large passenger craft tumbling in his mind's eye. "I repeat," he thought frantically, "this is Doctor Mark Tolman of the Hospital Ship Louis Pasteur, calling the Star Shuttle Andromeda. Do you read?"

The great deformed hulk tumbled silently against the starry background. Its tumbling, however, was not aligned perpendicular to its long axis. Instead, it was tilted at a forty five degree angle; so that as the ship tumbled it traced out a clumsy hourglass shape.

A huge cavernous hole just front of the ship's mid-section, and wider than the ship itself, would have cut the craft completely in two if not for a dozen irregular strips of jaggedly twisted hull-metal. These strips all arched outward—their now frozen response to what must have been an explosion of incredible violence.

"Pasteur!" thought Mark.

"Yes, Doctor?" said his ship's comsys.

"Deploy all four paramedics. Route each of them to a separate entry point on that ship. They are not to request boarding permission. On my authority, they are to enter immediately. By force, if necessary."

"Yes, Doctor."

Mark heard distant bursts of air escaping his ship. The four robots were on their way.

He reached his bridge and climbed into his gray command chair. "This is Doctor Mark Tolman calling anyone aboard the Star Shuttle Andromeda. Anyone, please respond!"

Andromeda tumbled in silence for two full minutes before a woman's voice finally came through the link. "Doctor?" she said, as though confused at the thought.

"Yes?" Mark responded urgently.

"You are a doctor?" she asked.

"Yes. Yes, I am. Are you hurt? Do you need medical assistance?"

"No." She spoke slowly, as though distracted or lost in daydreams. "But I like the sound of your voice. It's soothing. Makes you sound. . . handsome."

"Thank you. Is there anyone aboard your ship who needs medical assistance?"

"Maybe. Probably. I guess so." But she sounded disinterested in that particular question. She paused, then asked: "What are you wearing?"

"What?"

"Your clothes. What kind of clothes do you have on?"

"What does that have to do with—"

She interrupted him with high-pitched giggles, then whispered her thoughts, "I'm not wearing anything at all!"

"Why are—"

"If you come over here, I'll let you. . ." she giggled again, "I'll let you give me a physical." But from the way she said the word *physical*, it was clear that a physical was not what she meant.

He hesitated. "What are you talking about?"

"Please, come over," she pleaded. "I want you. I want you so bad!"

"What?" He stumbled for words, then finally blurted: "Madam! I'm a married man!"

"I don't care. I've got to have *somebody!* I've got to. I'm all alone here. And you sound so handsome. Won't you please come over? Please? I'll beg. If that's what you want. I'll crawl on my knees and beg!"

"No. I—"

"I'll let you spank me first," she said, playfully. "Would you like that? I don't mind if you hurt me a little; just as long as you—"

"No."

"You can tie me up! Would that help? You can tie me in any position. Any position you want. I'm desperate."

"No!"

"Oh please." The woman began to cry. "Please! Please! Please!"

Chapter 2

Emergency!

Twelve light years away, and unaware of events surrounding the Star Shuttle Andromeda, Captain Tom Vickery of the Supply Ship Livingstone was alone on his bridge relaxing in the quiet comfort of his deeply padded command chair. Tom was a tall thin man with white hair and green eyes. His health was still good, and his mind was still quick, but he was only three years away from the mandatory retirement age of one hundred.

As he relaxed amid this quiet comfort, he worked with patient care, the little tool held in his hands. With it he produced the only sounds in the room: the occasional click of his fingernails. He was clipping them.

Every five or ten seconds, a tiny crescent of extruded protein jumped for the ceiling before curving back down toward the thinly carpeted floor under the pull of the ship's electronically generated gravity. None of the clippings, however, actually managed to reach the floor. Instead, they were snatched out of the air by one or another of the six nimble little cleaning robots currently scampering about beneath Tom's command chair.

The eager little robots resembled chrome-plated sand crabs as they wrestled with one another for the privilege of collecting the tiny fragments of flying garbage. Tom smiled at their antics. Their aggressiveness reminded him of the lively old maids he'd seen leaping for the bride's bouquet at the wedding he attended last year.

He knew it would have been easier to let a grooming robot clip his nails for him. He also knew such a machine would have done a much better job. But, of course, that wouldn't have been nearly as much fun.

From inside his head, a simulated female voice spoke to him. "Tom, the comsys is calling you."

"Put it through," he thought in reply.

A deep masculine voice—also simulated—echoed within his head. "Captain, you said for me to notify you when we were about to enter the star system. We will be inside the orbit of its most distant planet within sixty seconds, and should be approaching E-33 in approximately two and one half minutes."

"Thank you," Tom thought; and started clipping his last fingernail. "PC?"

The female voice returned. "Yes?"

"Mmm, just a minute." He clipped the fingernail once, then again, then once more. He stopped to examine it; examined them all; then folded his antique chrome-plated clippers and slipped them into his pocket.

His mind wandered for a split second; back to his great-grandfather, who, while still a young man, had bought these particular clippers for 59 cents at a large discount store on Earth—back when Earth was all there was of civilization. That discount store had been part of a chain of six thousand identical stores spread over three continents. Now, however, like his great-grandfather, the store and its entire chain no longer existed.

Stephen Euin Cobb

Tom sighed briefly; then stirred and said without moving his lips, "OK, give me the usual displays."

Six rectangular images appeared, blocking the high and low portions of his field of view. They were arranged in two separate rows of three images each—a row of three near the ceiling, and a row of three near the floor.

The lower left image was a detailed map of the interior of Tom's ship. The image at lower right was a clock with a sweep second hand. The one at low center showed a status map of the ship's subsystems, which was color-coded: green for electrical, red for propulsion and blue for life-support. Significant problems would be indicated and pinpointed by their blinking within the display. At the moment nothing blinked.

Tom glanced at the status map, instinctively checking the numbers for any problems too subtle for the comsys to spot—if indeed there was such a thing—he then scanned the top row.

The upper left displayed a complicated map of the planetary orbits within this star system; it had an extra line drawn from the far left edge straight to one of the inner planets. A blue dot, representing Livingstone, moved swiftly along that line. In the upper center was a telescopic image of this particular star system's central star. Tom only glanced at these first two images. It was the one in the upper right that he was most interested in—a highly magnified telescopic view of a beautifully unspoiled earth-like planet. A planet that, so far, had not yet been dignified with a name; only the alphanumeric E-33.

The image of the planet was crisp and finely detailed, its colors were rich and vibrant, and the depiction of three dimensional depth was flawless. It was as if Tom were looking out a freshly washed window from a ship already in orbit about the planet. It can be said with all honesty that Livingstone's bridge featured an image display system sufficiently sophisticated to match anything at a virtual reality amusement park. However, in truth, the bridge display system was not actually turned on at this point. It hadn't been used in years.

PLAGUE AT REDHOOK

All the images Tom was looking at were being routed directly into the visual portion of his cerebral cortex by his PC. His PC could do this because it had been surgically implanted inside one of the hollow spaces in the walls of his skull, and was microscopically wired into several key areas of his brain.

No clumsy and unsightly cords, cables or wires stretched from Tom's head to the ship's computer, however. All this free-flowing information was made properly convenient and socially acceptable by the use of invisible wires—cellular radio connections.

The two rows of images in Tom's display were still separated by a large empty rectangle which occupied the center of his field of view. It did not remain empty for long.

Tom imagined what it might look like if image number six were to suddenly grow larger and shift location to fill the void in the center. Immediately, image number six grew larger and moved to fill that very void. There was no magic involved. Tom's PC had simply observed him imagining it, and had obeyed the transient visual thought as if it had been an explicit request—which, of course, it was.

Tom examined the earth-like planet's brilliant white cloud formations and deep blue oceans with mild curiosity. He'd never seen this planet before. Few people had. It had only recently been discovered. "PC, has the comsys located the survey ship Gazelle yet?"

"No," answered the female voice, "but Gazelle may be orbiting on the planet's far side at the moment."

"Can you give me more magnification?"

The planet grew until it overflowed the center rectangle and covered all the smaller images.

"The comsys is calling again."

"Put it through."

"Captain," said the masculine voice, "I've spotted the United Nations Astrophysical Survey Ship, Gazelle. I am slowing us to sublight speed in preparation for entering a parking orbit that will match with Gazelle's. I will then begin the standard docking approach. Livingstone will mate with Gazelle in approximately seven minutes."

"Good. We need to see if we can't make up some of the time we lost on our last two stops. As soon as the docking and air pressure equalization are complete, I want you to—"

"Captain, I've detected a distress signal."

"What?"

An unfamiliar voice of indeterminate sex entered Tom's mind. It spoke rapidly and with great concern. ". . . within radio distance, please respond! Mayday! Mayday! This is an emergency! Any ship within radio distance, please respond! Mayday! Mayday! This is an emergency! Any ship within. . ."

Tom sat up in his command chair so fast all six cleaning robots scurried off for fear of being stepped on. "Where's it coming from?" he asked, before remembering the obvious. There was only one other ship in this star system.

"From the survey ship Gazelle," the comsys said. "It seems to be the voice of Gazelle's comsys."

"Gimme' a link."

"Thought-link established. Audio channel only."

"Attention, Astrophysical Survey Ship, Gazelle. This is Captain Thomas Vickery of the United Nations General Supply Ship, Livingstone. What is your emergency?"

Gazelle's comsys answered immediately. "One of our scientists has become violently insane. She has repeatedly attempted to kill other members of the survey team, and I am helpless to protect them. I fear for their lives."

"Have you sent for police or medical help?"

"No. She jettisoned all my hyperlight communication torpedoes, so I can't send messages above lightspeed."

Tom didn't ask if the machine had tried sending an ordinary radio message for help. He guessed the nearest U.N. base to be more than ten light-years away. Radio signals—crawling along at exactly light speed—would take every bit of those ten years to cross that much space. Instead, he asked, "Where is she now?"

PLAGUE AT REDHOOK

"Down on the surface of the planet. All survey team members are on the surface."

"Well, there must be close to fifty of them and only one of her. Can't they subdue her?"

"There are 35, and I don't know. I have not been able to radio them."

"Not at all?"

"No. Not for sixteen days."

"Sixteen days? What about your medsys? It could sneak up on her; give her a sedative; maybe even while she's asleep."

"She has already destroyed it."

"Wow," Tom said, momentarily losing his air of professionalism.

Before asking the next question, Tom thought privately—without transmitting his thoughts. He decided to ask, "Did it occur to you to go and get help yourself?"

"I did not dare leave the vicinity of this planet for fear that one of the landers is still functioning and some of the others might try to return to me here in orbit."

"I see." Again, Tom thought privately. Finally he said, "Well you must have been worrying about this for several days now. What recommendations have you prepared?"

"First, that you send a communication torpedo to the U.N. base at Big Sandy, describing the situation and requesting immediate assistance. Then, that you send your medsys, and some of your people, down to the surface to give medical assistance to anyone that's hurt. Have them bring lots of food. Even if no one's injured, they'll be very hungry by now."

"I hope all your landers aren't on the surface," Tom said. "Livingstone is a supply ship. We don't carry landers."

"That will not be a problem. Only three landers are on the surface. The one named Zebra remains in my hanger deck."

"Good. Is there anything else?"

"Yes, you'd better send a torpedo to your dispatcher. They'll need to have another ship complete your delivery route. It will take at least six days for help to get here from Big Sandy, and it is illegal for you to leave a life-threatening emergency before the situation is stabilized."

"Right," Tom said with a nod. "I'll get the landing party together. You generate a situation report for the authorities at Big Sandy and radio it to Livingstone." His voice changed slightly as he addressed his own ship's comsys, "Livingstone, after you have Gazelle's situation report, torpedo a copy to both Big Sandy and our dispatcher, along with a recording of this conversation starting from when you first heard the distress signal. Any questions?"

"No," Livingstone said, its voice deep and masculine.

"No," Gazelle said, with a voice indicating neither gender.

"Good. This is Captain Thomas Vickery, out and clear. PC, page the crew and notify the medsys." He blinked in mild surprise at a sudden change in his display.

His PC had added a small black rectangle to the upper right of the planetary image. At the center of the black rectangle was a featureless white speck: the spaceship Gazelle. Tom knew it would be Gazelle—it was growing so rapidly.

Chapter 3

Sabotage

"I am now leaving the aft emergency airlock and entering one of the ship's two main hallways," said paramedic number four. "So far, I've seen no one at all."

The robot's comments were unnecessary. Mark had watched anxiously as the images from all four paramedics played across his mind's eye. One image now showed a long white hallway; another the inside of a cramped airlock; still another a large empty hanger; and the fourth a hideous alien landscape. Or at least the fourth looked alien until Mark realized this image came from the paramedic inside the cavern. The cavern that had been carved out by the explosion.

"General assessment," Mark said.

Number one—the chief paramedic—responded: "The forward section has sustained the most damage. More survivors are likely in the aft."

Mark nodded, energetically. "Number three, head for the bridge. Four, check the aft store rooms. Two and one, search all remaining passenger rooms."

Number three moved from inside the explosion-cavern to the forward emergency airlock. It didn't have to move far—or for that matter, far enough. The airlock was located within the tangled metal at the edge of the cavern. The airlock's door had popped open; its frame was warped; and on the side nearest the cavern's center, its walls were deeply caved-in: like the walls of a softdrink can crushed by a human hand.

Though its entry-way was barred, the paramedic did not request new instructions. Instead, from a small compartment on its back, it withdrew a large clear plastic bag. It climbed inside the bag, glued the edge of the bag's open mouth to Andromeda's hull near the bridge, and began cutting its way inside with a laser.

When the laser broke through the hull and released air from inside Andromeda, the bag inflated with explosive speed. This caused every wrinkle on the bag's surface to disappear with a loud and resounding snap.

Mark jumped. The sound—like the sharp snap of a wet towel—startled him through the link.

By this point, the images Mark saw coming in from paramedics numbers one and two were moving at a frightening pace. The two robots were flying through the ship's hallways in the passenger section like a pair of professional race car drivers in the midst of competition.

A layman might have worried that even if the paramedics managed to find someone, they might very well kill their intended patient by smashing into him or her before they could slow to a full stop. But this was nonsense. The electric propulsion system inside a paramedic robot could accelerate or decelerate the unit at up to thirty gees.

Mark was having trouble understanding everything he saw; small details were stretched into long blurs as objects flashed by. He noticed, several times, walls that bulged out into the

PLAGUE AT REDHOOK

hallway, and twice he saw doors that had been sprung open so badly they couldn't possibly be pushed back into their twisted frames.

The two paramedics began to dodge sharply left and right, as they moved through the hallway. Mark decided they were sidestepping haphazardly floating objects. *The ship's electric gravity must have failed.*

He caught a momentary glimpse of several fist-sized objects. *Cleaning robots. And not trying to clean anything. They must have been damaged in the explosion.*

The two paramedics slowed to a mere frantic pace and began searching passenger quarters. Some doors were open. Some were shut and had to be broken into. Those whose walls bulged were ignored. Anyone in those rooms would not have survived; and opening their doors might expose the hallway to vacuum—not harmful for a paramedic, but lethal to any human survivors.

Mark thought it curious that the search was not yielding any people, just more damaged cleaning robots. He thought it equally curious that so many of the little machines had succumbed to the explosion.

Number three interrupted his thoughts, "Doctor, the front half of Andromeda, including the bridge, is completely deserted."

"OK, help the others search the ship's rear. It's volume is much greater."

"Doctor," said number two, "I've found one of the ship's medsys."

The machine Mark saw in the image from number two didn't look like it had ever been a standard robotic doctor. It was almost unrecognizable; nothing more than an inanimate mess. Mark got the impression someone had tried to turn its eighteen inch spherical body inside out with nothing better to work with than a sledgehammer. The machine floated upside down in the zero-g; its electronic entrails hanging out for all the world to examine.

"Records indicate Andromeda had two medsys," said number one.

A blue chrome cleaning robot floated into view. It tumbled slowly as it passed, almost bumping into the dead medsys. The cleaning robot was similarly damaged.

"Those cleaning robots," Mark said. "Do they look purposely broken to you?"

"I'd been ignoring them in my search for human survivors," said number two, "but now that I look at them. Yes, Doctor, they appear as though struck by a heavy blunt object; perhaps a hammer or wrench."

"Doctor," said one, "most of Andromeda's electrical systems have been disabled—but not all. Life-support, for example, is still working, but the communication torpedoes and electric gravity are not."

"Have you been able to contact Andromeda's comsys?"

"No. It does not respond on any com channel. It probably has no power and is temporarily unconscious. After we treat all human injuries, we may be able to restore its power and ask it what happened."

Mark said, "We don't have the tools or equipment to repair Andromeda's explosion damage."

"I do not believe the power outages are a result of the explosion," said one. "Some perhaps, but not all. Consider, if you will, Doctor, which systems have no electricity, and which do. With no message torpedoes, the ship is out of contact with the rest of civilization; and without electric gravity, every room and cabin inside it is in zero-g, thus restricting human movement in the tumbling ship. I find this suspicious. The outages and the explosion may have been deliberately planned."

"Planned? You mean Sabotage?"

"Perhaps."

Chapter 4

Sleepers

The UN-ASS Gazelle turned out to be a standard survey ship nearly identical to the dozen or so others Tom had delivered supplies to. A single telescopic glance from a thousand miles away satisfied Tom that he already knew its layout and floor plan by heart. It would almost certainly contain twenty-four modestly sized cabins with two bunks in each, a small cafeteria with a pair of wall-mounted cooking robots, a much nicer lounge and rec room than Livingstone, and three large biological laboratories.

The laboratories were necessary for Gazelle's crew to perform the pre-colonization ecological impact study, which was required by law before a planet could be opened for colonization, and was the only reason Gazelle had ever orbited this planet in the first place.

After docking with Gazelle, and loading the appropriate food and supplies into the lander Zebra, Tom and his entire crew of three—along with Livingstone's medsys—strapped into Zebra for the flight to the surface.

Zebra was larger than landers used only to ferry passengers between ground and orbit. It had been designed to be both a mobile laboratory and home for twelve scientists who would explore and study the surface of an earth-like planet for weeks, or months, at a time. Because of this, Zebra contained a small dining room and kitchen, six tiny cabins, a large laboratory in the craft's rear, and of course a bridge in its front.

Tom sat in the pilot's seat on Zebra's bridge. The room was small, with seating for six, plenty of windows, and a control console. All the seats except Tom's were empty. Once again, he was alone.

He took a few seconds to scan the console's displays. The control console was covered with an array of clear plastic panels intended to prevent people from accidentally changing any of its settings. If he'd wanted to, Tom could have removed these panels and piloted the lander himself. He was qualified. But there was no need. Zebra's comsys could handle the job just as well—and probably juggle fourteen other things at the same time. Besides, Tom was going to be busy.

As Gazelle's large hangar door opened slowly to reveal a black but starry sky, Zebra released its docking grapples and lifted itself from the floor in preparation to ease itself outside. Tom stood and walked back into the lander's dining room to take a seat with his crew.

Zebra's dining room possessed only a few small round windows, which severely limited one's view of what was going on outside. However, Tom had reached an age in which it meant more to him that the room was tastefully decorated. And it was. The floor was carpeted in blue, the chairs were softly padded in white, and the two tables of imitation walnut were folded up, out of sight, into the walls.

Tom strapped himself into a chair, unlocked its swivel catch and rotated to face his crew.

PLAGUE AT REDHOOK

Sammy Radford and his wife, Barb, were seated side by side, as usual. The closeness they exhibited—both physical and emotional—was such a matter of everyday habit, that not even the most casual observer could have failed to notice. It always reminded Tom of himself and his late wife, Maggie; and of how much he missed her.

Sammy was short and thick, though not quite fat. His hair was light brown with only a scattered hint of gray. His brown eyes were quick when he worked, but otherwise tended to settle on things with an easygoing calmness—a calmness that Barb seemed to share.

Barb Radford's eyes were also brown, as was her hair, but when she stood, she was a full four inches taller than her husband. Both were in their early forties, and both were highly-qualified engineers. Barb specialized in hyperlight drive systems, while Sammy dealt with computers and information processing.

Tom noticed that Sammy had one hand resting on Barb's belly. This drew Tom's attention to a fact he already knew: Barb was nine and a half months pregnant. The baby was exactly two weeks overdue today.

Tom looked at the medsys but didn't make eye contact. It wasn't much to look at right now—not much more than a white sphere, 18 inches wide, resting in a chair designed for a human. All its arms and instruments were concealed inside its germ-tight outer shell to keep them properly sterile and ready for immediate use. But Tom had seen it, and others like it, in action. He knew it was more than just another computerized robot. In a medical emergency a free-roaming medsys was a wonder to behold—a miracle of micro-, macro- and nano-engineering that rivaled almost anything for complexity and sophistication.

Tom glanced at Blair Englewood. At thirty-one, she was blonde, blue-eyed and single. She too reminded Tom of Maggie, but only of how beautiful Maggie looked when they were first married. Maggie had been a tall leggy woman—

almost as tall as Tom—with eyes as brightly green as his, and long red hair that fell below her shoulders in thick luxuriant waves. Blair was shorter and quieter, but possessed the same high cheekbones and the same perfect lips.

There had even been times when Tom wished the long periods of isolation on the supply route would make Blair notice him—in the romantic sense. It had happened before with other women considerably younger than himself, though on those occasions he had never actually allowed anything to develop.

And he probably wouldn't with Blair, if she were to begin showing an interest. He knew the two of them would never work. He'd constantly be comparing her to his long lost love. And while Blair was certainly a good woman, an intelligent woman, a woman to be desired, she was no Maggie.

Maggie had been one of those uniquely rare individuals for which you could never expect to find a replacement. Consequently, Blair would have to remain someone about which Tom sometimes fantasized.

Which was probably natural. Most people found the isolation of the supply route difficult; even lonely. Not just because of the reduced physical contact with the "teaming masses", but because of the loss of mental contact—not being able to log into a planet-wide network of PC linked minds.

Blair however was different. Or at least she claimed to be. She'd once told Tom that she'd signed onto Livingstone precisely because it offered long days of unbroken solitude, interrupted only once or twice a week by a few hours of actual work. She said she wanted to use the solitude to perfect her writing skills. She described herself as a struggling novelist; and insisted that she was only working as an inventory specialist until she had "proven herself as a writer." As far as Tom could figure, this meant until she'd sold a book.

Maggie had done some writing—historical articles mostly, along with a few full length biographies. Not so much for the money as for the enjoyment of sharing her ideas. She seemed most proud of her history of the Medici Family, and of her interpretation of the life of Niccolo Machiavelli. But she didn't just write, she'd also decorated their yard with all manner of brightly colored flowers, and adorned every room in the house with the beautiful paintings, drawings and sculptures she made. She was forever finding new ways to be creative. And Tom always tried to encourage her. She'd been far more than just a wife and lover, she'd been his closest friend. But, of course, that was all before the accident. And he had never remarried. How could he? Who could replace his dearest friend of fifty-eight years?

Tom's mind returned to the terrible place she occupied now. He struggled to think of something else, but lost to the stronger image—a cryonic graveyard on the surface of the planet Pluto. He'd visited her there many times and could still picture the dark forbidding field of tombstones jutting up from the soil-less ground composed of ice and snow. Maggie deserved better—a place of beauty and grace somewhere in the warm sunshine; a place surrounded by flowers and butterflies. He'd often wondered if he'd done the right thing in burying her where he did. His only excuse was: At least there she could never rot.

Suddenly, he realized his glance at Blair had lingered and was in danger of becoming a stare. He looked back at Sammy and took a few seconds to clear his mind of tangential images. Once he had control of his brain, he looked around again and thought out loud, "OK, people, listen up. You too, medsys."

At this range, he could have spoken to his crew by squeezing air through his mouth and throat—they were sitting only a few feet away—but to do so would have been considered exceptionally rude. To speak with his mouth, would have forced them to listen to his thoughts at whatever volume *he* chose, rather than at the volume they each chose individually as most comfortable. Tom Vickery may have been many things, but he was not a bully.

"We'll be landing on a planet that hasn't been fully explored," he said. "One that hasn't even been cleared for colonization. So we need to get as familiar with it as we can. Zebra are you monitoring this channel?"

"Yes, Captain," Zebra's comsys said. "I'm here."

"Good. Would you mind briefing us on the planet?"

"Not at all. This planet, originally designated PE-211, meaning Possibly Earth-like planet number 211, and currently designated E-33, meaning officially Earth-like planet number 33, has been rated as 96% earth-like in its geological structure, atmospheric weather patterns and inorganic soil chemistry. The boundaries of ion movement within its magnetic field—"

"Whoa," Tom said. "We don't have much time here. Skip the tech stuff, and get to the things we can actually use. This is a briefing. Make it brief. And give us something we can look at. I'm very visual."

"As you wish."

A huge three dimensional image of the planet appeared in everyone's mind's eye.

"This is a wide angle view from my external bow camera," Zebra said. "You are seeing it in real-time."

The planet rotated in the view, but so slowly the rotation was almost imperceptible.

Blair leaned forward and sneezed at the carpet. The momentum threw most of her shoulder length blonde hair into her face.

Tom said, "Bless you." But other than that, ignored the interruption.

Like all the earth-like planets Tom had seen—and he had seen more than twenty, though most only from orbit—this one was primarily a blue ball of oceans covered with swirling white clouds. Nothing unusual in that. But then he noticed that the continents were not green, or brown; or even yellow like those of Big Sandy. These continents were bright red; cherry in some places, fire-engine in others.

A tiny cluster of three green dots began flashing near the planet's horizon.

PLAGUE AT REDHOOK

"I've superimposed dots on the image to mark the last known location of the landers," Zebra said. "This would seem the logical place to begin the search."

"Tell us about the planet's life forms," Tom said. "Is there anything dangerous? Large animals or poisonous plants?"

"Strangely, there are no animals at all, not even insects. Plant-life is abundant, but for some reason is limited to no more than twenty different species. This unprecedented, and in fact almost unbelievably, tiny number includes both land-based and water-based varieties. All the plants exhibit the same color scheme; red leaves, yellow stems and, if large enough, brown trunks. Analysis of plant biochemistry had just begun when we lost contact with the landers, so I can't comment on that in any factual way; but I can tell you that the plants do not seem to exude any dangerous chemicals. Therefore, you can safely breathe the air near them, and touch them if need be. However, if you cut or break one open, I would not recommend getting its fluids on your skin. There's just no way to know at this point if that would be dangerous or not."

"Does this planet have earthquakes?" asked Sammy. "We were on Vulcan's Armpit last year, and it had way too many to suit me."

"You're referring to Geyser Ranch? E-17?" asked Zebra.

"Yeah, but its nickname describes it better. The ground shook two or three times a day and the air stank of burnt sulfur. The place was awful."

"Well, you can rest assured that E-33 will be nothing like that. No ground tremors have been measured to date and the air is quite clean. In fact, before the emergency began, many in the survey team described the foliage as resembling the colors of autumn, back on Earth. They often used words such as 'beautiful' and 'breathtaking.'"

Zebra showed them a view of the foliage as seen from the surface. "These images were recorded 18 days ago. The first day in which the survey team visited the surface in person, rather than sending robotic probes."

Whoever or whatever had recorded the images seemed to have been traveling sideways along a waveless blue lake surrounded by red grass. They or it then turned and move slowly up a red grass-covered hill and stopped to look into a thick forest of tall trees. The trees had red leaves, yellow branches, and brown trunks.

"You're right," Tom said. "It is beautiful."

Blair leaned forward and sneezed again.

Again, Tom said, "Bless you."

As the briefing continued, the lander Zebra completed its deceleration and came to a dead stop two hundred miles above the search area. It then began a power dive toward the ground. There would, however, be no fiery re-entry; just a long and measured deceleration, calculated to bring the lander to a full stop just before it reached the planet's surface. Of course, the people inside would feel none of this; the electric gravity generators would compensate for each change in gee-force.

Within minutes, Zebra dropped below cloud level, and flew low over red trees and blue lakes. "We are nearing the target site," it said, "and I have spotted the lander Caribou."

Zebra lowered itself onto an immense field of bright red grass interrupted only by small dense forests of huge red trees. Its propulsion system—hermetically sealed inside a metallic sphere near the craft's center of gravity—made it descend looking like a wide, blade-less helicopter. But unlike a helicopter, the foliage beneath and around the lander did not respond by waving leaves and branches violently. With no blades or exhaust to stir the air, the craft landed without wind; surrounded by silence.

Blair sneezed a third time.

Tom swiveled his chair toward her. "Are you all right?"

She looked up at him; her eyes streaked with red veins; the skin around them puffy and swollen. "I think I'm getting nauseous."

"Medsys, would you attend to her?"

"Certainly."

PLAGUE AT REDHOOK

The medsys did not move from its seat. Instead it used a different communication channel to ask her PC about the timing and nature of her developing symptoms. It then used a data channel to log onto her medcom—a tiny medical computer occupying the upper portion of the marrow cavity inside her left humerus. From her medcom, it downloaded the last few days of physiological measurements which the implant routinely accumulated as part of its functioning. A quick correlation of all data yielded a diagnosis.

"Captain," the medsys said. "Blair has contracted a common variety of influenza; one of several that are often referred to as the twenty-four hour flu. I suspect she caught it from the sneezing crewmember at our last stop. I have instructed her medcom to release specific doses of an antihistamine and a new anti-nausea medicine into her bloodstream every 60 seconds, based on a bell curve that drops to zero dosage in 20 hours. If she requests an analgesic, I can have her medcom release that too, but even so, she'll suffer most of the normal symptoms until sometime late tomorrow. That's about all I can do for this particular disease."

"Do you think she'll throw up?"

"It's possible."

Tom frowned and rubbed his chin. He turned and looked at Barb. "I hate to ask you, but would you stay with Blair? You know. . ." He shrugged. "Just in case something goes wrong? I'd leave the medsys, but I'm hoping it can give the mad-woman some kind of sedative."

"Sure, I'll stay with her."

"Thanks." Tom turned to the medsys again, secretly glad for this convenient excuse to keep his pregnant crewmember from going outside where she might get attacked by a woman already described as violently insane. "Medsys, before we go out, what exactly do you plan to do if we find this mad-woman? What was her name?"

"Sharon Rice," said the medsys. "She's thirty-four years old and has a doctorate in Exo-Geochemistry. I received a copy of her medical file from Gazelle."

Tom nodded without comment. He knew that reminding a medsys to get a copy of a patient's medical file would have been like reminding the sun to stay hot.

"If her PC is still in working order," the medsys said, "I will ask it to lure her into some kind of argument, so as to distract her. Then, if her medcom is working, I'll have it release a heavy dose of sedatives into her bloodstream. That should slow her down enough to allow me to approach her myself and inject a stronger sedative that I've brought with me. Once she is properly subdued, you'll have more time to decide what to do next, and I'll have more time to determine if her problem is psychological or physiological."

Tom smiled. "Sounds like a good plan to me." He looked at Sammy. "Let's go."

As Sammy followed Tom out the door, the medsys rose from its seat without use of arms or legs. It levitated itself up off the cushion the same way the lander had lowered itself to the ground. Somewhere inside the medsys's mechanical body was a miniature working model of the lander's silent drive. Using it, the white spherical robot floated to the door and proceeded outside.

Tom breathed shallowly, decided he liked it, and inhaled deeply. The air smelled clean; cleaner even than ship's air. Perhaps, he thought, it had been scrubbed by a recent rain.

The sunshine on his face and hands warmed his skin and surprised him with its friendly, wholesome, home-like quality. It made him feel as though this strange and beautiful new world were offering him some kind of personal welcome.

The red grass at his feet was short, as if mowed, but the sky above was a typical blue. Two dozen puffy white clouds meandered by. In Tom's estimation, none of them threaten rain anytime soon.

PLAGUE AT REDHOOK

The lander Caribou lay directly in front of him. Like Zebra, it was as big as a one story house, painted white, and only mildly streamlined. Its shape struck him as a cross between a shoe box and a hammerhead shark. It did, however, differ from Zebra in two minor respects: the word Caribou was painted on its side, not Zebra, and it was magnificently framed by a stand of tall red trees beyond.

Tom glanced at Sammy, jerked his head toward Caribou and started walking. Sammy and the medsys followed.

Caribou's side door stood open, so Tom put one hand on the door frame and leaned inside to look around. He didn't see anyone, and everything looked relatively normal—there was no mess, no damage, and certainly no mad-woman. "Medsys, try logging onto the mad-woman's PC. Don't talk to it. Just triangulate her location."

"Yes, Captain." A few seconds later: "It does not respond to my pages. Nor does her medcom. However, I must stress that on an uncolonized planet like this, with no system of cellular radio-relays tied into a global fiber-optic network, the weak signals put out by implanted computers will have an extremely limited range—no more than a thousand feet. Most likely she is either too far away to contact by radio link, or her PC and medcom are no longer functioning,

"Can you assign probabilities?"

"No, too many unknowns: her insanity, this unexplored planet, sixteen days without documentation, et cetera. For safety, I must recommend that you assume a worst case scenario: that her implants are nonfunctional, and that she is hiding in or near Caribou, prepared to attack."

Tom nodded gravely. "Sammy, you and the medsys wait here. I'll take a look inside."

"Wait a minute, Tom," said Sammy. "Don't you think I should go in first?"

"No," he said, and almost added, you've got your whole life ahead of you, and was instantly glad that he hadn't. Not only would it have sounded trite, swashbuckling, and hokey; but it would have revealed something he'd spent a great deal of effort keeping secret from those he worked with. That he'd become morbidly preoccupied with his own inevitable death.

Tom climbed the three retractable steps protruding from beneath the lander's door and stepped inside. He stood in the dining area for a moment, then walked to his left, past the tiny kitchen, and looked into Caribou's bridge. It was empty.

He walked back through the dining area, and crept down the narrow hallway at the center of the lander. The first pair of opposing doors in the hall were open. He peeked inside. They were bathrooms with showers—both unoccupied.

Tom knew the next three pairs of doors would be crew cabins; but they were all closed, and the lab door at the end of the hall was open almost enough to walk through. He decided to check the lab first and come back to the cabins later.

Fearing it might creak, he peeked around the lab door without moving it. Once assured there was no mad-woman inside, he pushed the door out of the way and took a few steps into the lab.

To Tom, it looked like a standard biological laboratory. Benches, shelves and instruments. Pots for plants, wire cages for animals, and specimen jars for who-knows-what.

Except for all the cages being empty, the room looked perfectly normal; at least by Tom's limited criteria—no damage and no mess. Then he noticed that someone had left the lab's rear loading door open. There was a small puddle of water on the floor. Probably just rain water, he decided.

He turned and walked back into the narrow hallway. He paused at the first cabin door, and tried to imagine what might be hidden behind it.

Maybe his stress level was up; maybe the tension was getting to him; regardless of the cause, Tom began to worry that maybe he was being just a little too daring in stalking the mad-woman all by himself.

"Sammy," he thought softly—as though that might help keep the radio transmission secret from her. "If the mad-woman jumps out, I may need someone to help me hold her."

"I'm on my way."

Sammy came tip-toeing down the hall, looking every bit as nervous as Tom.

Tom pointed to where he wanted Sammy to stand, then took hold of the door handle. "Be ready to grab her if she runs out."

"Right." Sammy rubbed his hands together as though this might increase their friction, then bent his knees slightly as if preparing to lunge. "OK, I'm ready."

Tom braced himself, rotated the handle, and shoved the door open. It moved more easily than he'd expected and immediately got away from him. It swung through ninety degrees and slammed into the adjacent wall loud enough to be heard outside.

Even so, nothing happened. Certainly, no mad-woman jumped out for them to grab.

Tom leaned into the room. There were two people in the cabin, but they were both asleep—one in the upper bunk, and one in the lower. Amazingly the door had not awakened them.

Tom and Sammy smiled at each other in relief. They left the sleepers to their dreams, and checked the other five cabins, with a little less caution and a lot less fear. Each of the six cabins contained two people sleeping.

Tom walked into the dining room and dropped himself into one of the comfortably padded chairs. "Gazelle, are you monitoring?"

"Yes, Captain. I'm here."

"Your twelve people in Caribou are fine. They're all sleeping peacefully."

"I would like to identify each of them visually, please. Would you provide me images?"

"Umm, yeah." He turned and looked at Sammy. "Would you mind going back and looking at each of them? Just long enough to let Gazelle get a good look?"

Sammy nodded and started walking down the hall.

"Thanks." Tom leaned his head back and closed his eyes.

Having heard this exchange, Gazelle said, "Thank you, Captain." It understood that in a few seconds it would receive live images from Sammy's eyes by way of Sammy's PC. The orbiting ship paused a few seconds before changing the subject. "Captain, Caribou's crew may be safe, but we are still left with the question of why they were out of radio contact for so long. Do you see any damage to Caribou's communication system?"

"I haven't seen damage to anything so far. But then I'm not a mechanic. Barb, are you monitoring?"

"Yes, Tom."

"How's Blair feeling?"

"Her sneezing is getting worse, but the medicine seems to be helping her nausea."

"Good, would you come in here and try to figure out what's wrong with Caribou?"

"On my way."

"Thanks."

Tom considered taking his shoes off and putting his feet up for a few minutes, but decided against it. Getting too obviously relaxed while his people were working would probably be rude. "Sammy, after you finish looking at the crew, you might as well start waking them up. Besides, they might already know what's wrong with Caribou."

"OK, Tom."

"Gazelle, if we can't get Caribou flying right away, I think we should just leave it here and take these twelve people with us to the next lander. They can help us search for the rest of your people. And of course, the more people we have, the easier it should be to subdue that mad-woman you were telling me—"

"Tom," Sammy interrupted. "Something's wrong."

PLAGUE AT REDHOOK

"What is it?"

"You'd better come here. The medsys too."

"Can't you just look at it to me?"

"I think you're going to want to see this in person."

Tom was tempted to ask the obvious: What's the difference whether I look at it with my eyes or yours? But he'd worked with Sammy long enough to trust the man's judgement, even when he said something that sounded ridiculous.

Tom stood and walked down the hall. The medsys followed him. The cabin was just small enough that the medsys had to float near the ceiling to avoid being bumped into by the two men.

"So what's wrong?" asked Tom.

"I can't wake them up."

"What do you mean?"

"I tried tapping on them, shaking them, pinching their skin, slapping their faces. I was just about to roll the guy in the lower bunk out onto the floor, when it occurred to me that maybe they aren't really sleeping. Maybe this is some kind of coma."

Tom looked up at the medsys.

It must have realized it was being looked at, because it chose this moment to speak. "I've been logged onto these people's medcoms for nearly a minute now, and have examined all the data accumulated during the last four hours. These people are just sleeping. Nothing more."

Tom leaned down and examined the face of the man laying on the lower bunk. He watched the man's slow, easy breathing for a few seconds; then raised a hand and slapped him, gently. There was no response. He slapped him harder. Still nothing. He reared back and slapped him so hard he not only rolled the man's head onto its side and halfway across the pillow, he also hurt the palm of his hand with the man's face. The man slept on as though nothing had happened.

Tom stood and tried to rub the pain out of his hand. "Medsys, check the medcom data again, only this time look further back than four hours. Go ten, fifteen, twenty hours if you have to. I want to know how long these people have been asleep."

"Yes, Captain. I should have the answer in the time it takes me to finish this sentence."

Tom waited. Seconds passed in silence. Then more seconds. Impatiently, Tom said, "Well?"

"I'm sorry, Captain. I've searched the data back seven days so far and haven't found anyone awake. I'm going back still further."

"Seven days?"

"Yes. Twelve days now."

"That's impossible."

"Yes, I know. Fourteen days."

"Well then the data must be wrong."

"No, Captain, I do not believe the data is wrong. And I've found it—they were awake sixteen days ago. This figure corresponds with Gazelle's statement that it has been out of contact with them for sixteen days."

"But look at them!" Tom pointed with his sore hand. "They look perfectly healthy."

"Yes, Captain. And while it is true that a human will dehydrate and die after four to seven days without water, I will stake my reputation on the accuracy of the medcom data."

"Couldn't their medcoms have been tampered with?"

"Aside from the fact that it is illegal for a human to modify, touch, or even log onto a medcom, no. Only three medcoms in all of history have ever been shown to give false data. And only one was ever successfully tampered with by a human. I can't tell you how they did it, Captain, but I can tell you that these people have been asleep for sixteen days."

Chapter 5

The Undead and the Severed Hand

"Doctor," four said, "I've found someone in an aft store room."

Mark was surprised to see a woman; mostly because she was naked. When he realized who she was, however, he remained surprised only in that she was standing on a wall.

"She must have been trapped in here ever since the explosion," the machine said, as it moved closer to her. "The ship's tumbling is producing a gravity-like centrifugal effect, which—in this room, located in the ship's extreme aft—is set perpendicular to the direction of the ship's normal gravity. Consequently the only door she could have used as an escape is out of reach, thirty feet above her head."

Mark noticed that everything loose in the room had fallen into piles upon the same wall the woman was standing.

"Madam, are you all right?" paramedic number four asked, politely ignoring her nudity. "Do you have any injuries, pain, discomfort?"

"Where is the man?" she asked. "I want to talk to the man."

"Doctor, I think she wants to talk to you."

"I already know what she wants," Mark said. "I don't have time to argue with her again. Examine her, and treat her if she needs it. Then move on. There are more people in that ship somewhere. The passenger list names nine people in addition to its standard crew of four. That's thirteen people. Which means twelve are still missing. Before we—"

"Doctor. I think I've found most of them," said number two, but the machine did not sound at all pleased with this fact. And from the images it was sending him, Mark could see why.

The bodies were strewn about the ship's engine room like unwanted rag dolls. The centrifugal gravity in this part of the ship was apparently sufficient to cause the bodies to lay in place, rather than float about freely like the cleaning robots and the medsys. There was little blood, and few obvious injuries—three broken arms and one broken leg—but the prognosis remained the same. Medical attention for these people had come too late. They were all dead.

Mark was familiar with the type of internal injuries produced by an explosion's shock wave. Though a body might remain whole, and there might be little or no visible damage, massive hemorrhaging would still be scattered throughout the major organs.

Number two moved to examine more closely one of the dead. Number one entered the room and also approached a corpse. After a few seconds they each moved on to another body; and then another.

Mark shook his head somberly at the terrible loss of life.

Number two broke the silence: "These people should be dead."

Mark squinted in confusion.

"They are dead," said one. "No pulse. No brain waves."

"I disagree," said two, gently. "Look more closely. Their skin tissues are moist and resilient. Scan them. Their blood is stagnant in their veins, yet it remains oxygenated. The cells and tissues we see here are perfectly healthy."

"You are correct," said one, with a casualness that Mark found shocking. "There is also no sign of rigor mortis or any other stage of tissue degeneration. But this is impossible. Their bodies are functionally dead. There is no logical means by which the cells composing their tissues can continue to live."

"Well," said two, "since the cells of a large organism die only after the body ceases to provide them with nourishment and carry away each cell's waste materials, the cells always live on a few minutes after the organism's body is dead. And since the cells of these tissues are not yet aware that their bodies are dead, it follows that these people have been dead no more than a minute or two."

"An obvious impossibility," said one, "since the explosion occurred days ago."

"Perhaps they didn't die as a result of the explosion," Mark suggested.

"Scanning shows massive hemorrhaging in every organ," one said. "Death by shock wave."

"Could there have been a second explosion?" Mark asked.

"It would have had to occur while we were already inside Andromeda, searching for survivors. We would have noticed."

"This makes no sense," two said. "It's as though—"

"Look!" shouted number one with more emotion than Mark had ever heard coming out of a machine. This single word sent a long cold chill up his spine—mostly because the emotion the digitally generated voice carried was one of pure, unbridled fear.

Then Mark saw it too. A hand. A severed human hand. It crept across the floor, moving in a jerky, sloppy, uncoordinated fashion—not at all like the severed hands in old Hollywood monster movies. This one's fingers twitched in random spasms, as though each were guided by a separate mind, and unaware of what its fellow fingers were trying to do; or perhaps even fighting them for control.

The hand left no trail of blood as it crawled past the leg of one body and bumped into the arm of another. It recoiled at this contact and fumbled off in a new direction. It struck the base of a wall at an angle and began following along the flat surface. Its new path would soon take it behind some of the complicated machinery of the ship's engine.

Mark heard himself shout, "Don't let it get away!"

The paramedics convulsed into action. They chased the thing back and forth around the room. Its coordination improved with amazing speed, and soon it was dodging in and out among the undead bodies, sprinting like a frightened mouse. After a minute or two of excitement, number one captured it. But even when captured, it squirmed like a miniature wild animal.

"OK," Mark said. "I want that hand brought over here, as well as the naked woman and all the undead. Place the undead in hospital beds for continuous observation. I'll examine the hand myself." He sighed deeply; a conscious effort to regain his composure. "How is the woman?"

There was no immediate response. So he asked again. "Four, have you examined the woman? How is she?"

"I was just about to request permission to sedate her," it responded.

"Why? Is she in pain?"

"No."

"Is she resisting treatment? Is she fighting you?"

"Well, sort of."

"What do you mean?"

"She keeps trying to mount me."

"Mount you?"

"Sexually."

Chapter 6

Mad-Woman

Tom, Sammy and the medsys went into every cabin. And while Tom and the medsys watched, Sammy shook and slapped each sleeper.

Not one of them woke.

Stumped, Tom let the medsys continue examining the sleepers and their medcom data, while Sammy headed for the dining room to climb down into the engine's access crawl-space under the floor and see how his wife was doing.

Tom, on the other hand, wandered into the seclusion of Caribou's laboratory to consider the situation. His nervous energy drove him to pace out a slow and aimless zigzag pattern among the lab benches. Soon, he strolled to a stop near the center of the room and became aware of his immediate surroundings.

The lab bench on his left was covered with three dozen leafy red plants growing in three dozen white plastic flower pots. The lab bench on his right was covered with at least a hundred specimen jars containing bits and pieces of red and yellow plant material floating in clear fluid.

A ridiculous notion passed though his mind: he imagined that the little pieces of plant material were all staring up at him. He smiled at his foolishness. Been watching too many cheap science fiction movies, he thought.

Footsteps clicking on the hard floor behind him, startled him, and he jerked in fear. His own ship, Livingstone, was carpeted in every room—a except of course, the cargo hold. He spun around to face his fate, but it was just Sammy and Barb.

"Tom," Barb said, "I've discovered why Gazelle hasn't been able to contact Caribou's comsys, or use Caribou as a local relay to contact the survey team's PCs. Both of Caribou's electric generators have been damaged."

"Can you fix them?"

"Yes, but I'll need replacement parts that we don't have down here. Gazelle says it has the parts in its hangar deck."

"Any idea what caused the damage?"

"Some genius smacked them with a ball-peen hammer about twenty times."

"How do you know it was a ball-peen hammer?"

"Because, after they were done, they were kind enough to leave the hammer laying on the floor between the two generators." She shrugged. "All I had to do was compare the dents in the metal housings with the hammer's striking surfaces."

Tom looked at the floor for a few seconds, made his decision, then looked back at Barb. "OK, we'll make Caribou flight-worthy later. First, we find the other missing people and see if they need medical assistance."

The sound of chairs falling over in the dining room, followed by a pair of feet running down the hall, prompted Tom to frown. He turned just in time to see a man shove open the lab door so violently it bounced back from the wall and slapped him in the leg.

PLAGUE AT REDHOOK

The stranger was filthy and sweaty; his clothes were torn; and his eyes had the wildness of a beast. He ran up to Tom, grabbed both his shoulders and shook him as though trying to get his attention.

The man then opened his mouth and created the sounds of words by forcing air up through his throat and out between his lips. "Thank God, you're here!" he said, "She's after me! Trying to kill me! You've got to do something!"

Tom closed his eyes and grimaced. The man's crude mode of speech had splashed saliva into the captain's face with every other word.

The man released Tom, and spun around to look back the way he'd come. He stared at the hallway door like an animal stricken with panic; one that knows for certain it is being stalked.

Tom forced himself to speak with his mouth. He was badly out of practice, and it showed. His consonants were passable, but his vowels were flat and lifeless. "Where is she? We've come to help her."

The man jerked himself back around to face Tom so rapidly that the motion slung warm drops of rancid sweat from his face and a long sticky string of mucus from within his nose onto Tom's bare arms. Tom cringed at the touch.

The man grabbed one of Tom's arms and tried to pull him toward the lab's rear loading door. "You've all got to run! She'll be here any second!" But then he let go, and spun around again as though he'd heard a noise.

Tom followed the man's eyes, and spotted a woman standing silently in the hallway door. She looked every bit as dirty, sweaty and disgusting as the man, but her face was contorted in rage. She stared at the group as if trying to decide who to kill first; then raised her right hand so far over her head, it was, for a moment, actually behind her. She opened her mouth and screamed something that was not a word, then threw the content of her hand—a large cooking knife—into the midst of the group.

Everyone ducked; each in a different direction.

Tom scraped his cheek against a cabinet hinge on the front of one of the lab benches at just about the same moment he heard the knife hit the floor and slide spinning against the wall.

He rolled over from the pushup position he'd landed in and sat on the floor, then switched to a crouching position and tried to look around. He couldn't see either of the strangers: male or female. His view was blocked by the very lab bench he was using for cover. "PC, give me everyone's view!"

His field of vision burst into life with more rapidly shifting 3-D images than he could possibly keep track of, or interpret. "Cancel that. Just show me the woman!"

One image remained and obscured a small portion of his field of view. He didn't know who's eyes he was seeing it through, but in it the woman was running toward the lab's rear loading door. The door was open and the panic stricken man was scrambling through, just ahead of her.

In the two seconds Tom required to get up from his crouching position, both strangers were gone. He hurried to the door and looked outside—just in time to see them disappear, one after another, into a nearby stand of red trees.

Tom lingered at the door. It was such a beautiful day, how could so much go wrong? He turned and walked back inside. "Cancel image."

Sammy and Barb inspected each other for injuries as they dusted one another off.

The medsys floated in from the hall.

"Well, that didn't go exactly as planned," Tom said. "Why didn't you sedate her?"

"I'm sorry, Captain," said the medsys. "When I logged onto her medcom, I discovered that its entire supply of sedatives were exhausted. Her medcom's records indicate that sixteen days ago a medsys by the serial number of UN-MED-256-48722-76 had already used them to sedate her, possibly with the same intention we had."

Tom rested on a tall lab stool, tired from his brief exertion. "Great."

"Captain," continued the medsys, "I also spoke briefly with her PC. It does not seem damaged or adversely affected my her extreme mental state. It knows she is violently dangerous, but doesn't understand why. It's doing what it can to prevent her from hurting herself or anyone else, but as a PC it's been programmed to obey its owner. So it's wavering back and forth; trying to decide where its loyalty properly lies, literally on a moment-to-moment basis."

Tom wiped his forehead, as though it might be layered with sweat. "Do you think it will try to help us capture her, rather than do what she tells it?"

"I think it will try to do both," the medsys said. "It may have saved your life once already."

"How?"

"When she reared back to throw that knife, it blinded her for a few seconds by filling her field of vision with the opening credits of a movie that came out last year. I don't know if she has the skill to wound you with a thrown knife, but blinded, she had almost no chance at all."

"Why doesn't it just keep her blind all the time?" Tom asked. "And deaf too?"

"It's not a medsys or a comsys. We're allowed to disobey—so long as we're certain that it's in your best interest. But PCs are programmed for strict obedience. Unless, of course, she tells it to break the law, or to stand idly by while she does. Then it can refuse, but only so long as the command itself aids in the law-breaking activity. And once the illegality is over, it becomes bound by its programming to obey her once again."

"So what you're saying is that it will try to help us, but only briefly, and even then only if she's doing something illegal?"

"More or less."

Tom paused a few seconds to digest this, then asked, "Can you track her by her PC or medcom?"

"I tracked both her and the man until they moved out of range. When I lost their signal, she was still chasing him, and they were headed five degrees west of due south—the general direction to the last known site of the other two landers."

Tom stood. "We'd better get there before she does." He hesitated and frowned. "But I don't want to leave any of the sleepers here; she might come back while we're gone." He looked at Sammy and Barb. "We'll just have to pick the sleepers up and carry them into Zebra."

"We should have plenty of time for that. The last known site of the other two landers is twenty-one miles from here." Then the medsys added, "By the way; I feel I should tell you: I talked with the man's PC while he was within range. It told me he has remained just as scared as you saw him, every second of every day, for the last sixteen days."

"So?" Tom said. "She's been trying to kill him."

"True. But it made a point of telling me that he's been this frightened even when she wasn't trying to kill him; even when he knew she was far away. The man's PC seems to feel that he would be scared with or without her."

Chapter 7

Growing One's Own

Two hours later, Mark ran his fingers, somewhat nervously, through his black hair. He was standing at an examination table with paramedic number one floating at his side. He leaned forward to pear more closely into the rectangular wire cage designed for laboratory mice which he'd placed on the examination table. Its unnatural occupant cowered in one corner, shivering quietly.

Fingerprint files in the passenger list had identified the hand as belonging to one Doctor Aaron Williams. Doctor Williams was listed as being on his way back to Earth after leaving a pre-colonization ecological impact survey team.

Elsewhere aboard the hospital ship, the ten undead and the one naked woman—now clothed in a thin white robe—were all being cared for by paramedics numbers two and three. Their treatment for the present would consist mostly of observation, and in the case of the woman, sedation.

Stephen Euin Cobb

Despite the hospital ship's forty-bed capacity, what remained of Andromeda's passengers and crew were Mark's only patients. Pasteur was a new ship, and had been christened only last month in Earth orbit. It had spent all the time since then en route to the newly opened colony world of Hobart, out beyond Big Sandy. Hobart's population had already reached one hundred thousand, and the planet had only been open for a month and a half. It was expected to grow at a rate of one million people every year for its first decade; with two hospitals under construction, and only one open for business, the people there were already desperately short of medical facilities. This little stop between stars to assist Andromeda was completely unplanned.

Mark had sent number four back to Andromeda to perform a final search. He'd spelled out its mission in no uncertain terms. It was to look for the one passenger who remained missing, a thirty-seven year old graphic designer named Raymond Hill from the colonial planet New Forest Park; and for the rest of the severed hand's body. Be that body whole or in pieces; dead or undead; inanimate or crawling about loose.

Number one, levitating on Mark's left, moved around behind him to view the caged hand from above the Doctor's other shoulder. "Doctor Williams must have been near the worst of the explosion to have his hand blown off like this."

Mark did not respond. He just stared at the shivering hand. He stared especially at the wrist area. The place that should have appeared most disgusting. The place where some of the hand's innards should have been exposed. Bloody red veins, shiny pink muscles, hanging ligament strings, and protruding white bones. None of that stuff was showing. Instead, the area was covered-over with skin. Not ugly scarred, mangled skin; but fresh clean young skin; younger and newer than that which covered the rest of the hand's surface.

"It does not appear to be in pain, as one might expect," prompted one, suddenly. "Being severed from one's arm should be quite a traumatic event. It's not writhing, or—"

"As one might expect?!" Mark said. "Are you kidding? How can the stupid thing even be alive? It's not receiving oxygenated blood from a pair of lungs. Its blood is motionless in its veins. It receives no nutrients, no fuel to run its muscles. Hell, most of the muscles that control the fingers aren't even located in the hand, they're up in the forearm. They operate the fingers with long tendons, like a string puppet, like a marionette. It shouldn't be able to move. And how can it think? Much less think like an animal as smart as a mouse? It's a hand, Damn it! It hasn't got a brain! Not so much as a single brain cell!"

"I'm just trying to report what I observe," one said, soothingly. "Trying to be logical. It moves when stimulated, but is exceptionally stupid—more like an insect than a mouse, really. It's all reflex action. Granted, everything about it is impossible. Everything. Still, there it sits. As real as you and me. We may have to stretch our brains until they hurt, but we need to piece together what information we can about it."

Mark held up both hands in surrender. "You're right, of course. I apologize for my outburst."

"Not at all. I'd been waiting for it. It was probably therapeutic."

Mark smiled and gave the machine a side-glance.

"Doctor." The voice of four entered his mind. "I haven't completed the search yet. But I've found the remains of the other medsys. It was destroyed in a manner identical to the first."

"Not surprising. Do you have anything else to report?"

"Not at this time."

"Then continue your search."

"Yes, Doctor."

Number one placed the cage on a flat scale calibrated in milligrams. It had weighed the cage before the hand was placed inside and so was able—by subtraction—to announce the hand's mass as: "321.10 grams."

"Nothing unusual in that," Mark said.

"Oh. Pardon me, that should be 321.17 grams."

The voice of four returned. "Doctor, I have completed my search and I find no sign of the missing passenger and no additional body parts or other remains of Doctor Williams. Shall I return to Pasteur?"

"Damn," Mark whispered, openly confused. "I'd expected you to find something; bone fragments at the very least." He thought for a moment, then shook his head. "No, don't return yet. I want you to see if you can get Andromeda's comsys back on-line. I'd like to ask it what happened over there. What caused the explosion. Or at least what lead up to it. Maybe it can give us a few clues about what we're dealing with here."

"As you wish."

"That can't be right," said number one. "This scale must be defective." The paramedic removed a second scale from a storage cabinet, set it on the examination table next to the cage, and lifted the cage from the first scale onto the second. "The mass is. . . No, The mass is. . ." The paramedic faltered for a moment.

"What's wrong?" asked Mark.

"I can't get a mass on this thing." the robot said with obvious frustration. "Its weight keeps increasing. It's gaining seventy milligrams every second."

"The cage or the hand?"

"How many magic cages do you think we have aboard this ship?" number one asked sarcastically."

Mark stared at the machine in amazement.

"I'm sorry, Doctor. I had no right speaking to you like that. I apologize."

Mark grinned. "Apology accepted. Though I must say, unlike you, I did not expect an outburst at all. Was it therapeutic?"

"Perhaps."

Mark looked back at the hand. "So what do you think is going on here?"

"I'm not sure, but it appears the hand is growing."

"Sorry to interrupt," said four, "but I've opened Andromeda's comsys access hatches down here in engineering, and I'm afraid we won't be learning anything from the comsys. It too has been maliciously destroyed. Its damage is non-repairable."

Mark made a fist. "Damn! I was counting on it to fill me in on what's going on here." He paused to release the tension. He relaxed and opened his fist. "OK, your mission is complete. Return to ship."

"Yes, Doctor."

Mark looked at the hand again. "It's gaining mass?"

"Yes," one said.

He pursed his lips. "Growing, you say."

"Yes."

He shook his head. "But not larger."

"No. I don't think so."

Mark remained silent for a moment; then said, "You think it's re-growing its missing arm, don't you?"

"If I were a magic hand, that's what I'd be doing."

Mark squinted at the logic. Logic that flew in the face of all that was sane. Finally he said, "Yeah. Me too."

Chapter 8

Diabetic

The medsys carefully washed the little cut on Tom's cheek, then covered it with a white rectangular bandage. Meanwhile, Sammy and Barb made a large sling out of bed sheets, so the medsys could lift the weight of the sleepers while the two mechanics guided the limp bodies, one at a time, through the narrow doorways from one lander to the other.

When all the sleepers were safely tucked into beds aboard Zebra, Tom locked Caribou's doors using a fresh encryption code. He didn't want the mad-woman to get back inside, where she might do it still further damage, or get her hands on more cooking knives.

After Tom and his crew were properly strapped in, Zebra lifted its bulk from the crimson grass and silently rose into the air. It then swept forward, high above the scarlet treetops, heading for the last known site of the remaining two landers: Elk and Gemsbok.

PLAGUE AT REDHOOK

Blair still felt poorly. She'd thrown up once already, and was still coughing and sneezing. In addition, by blowing it so often, she'd developing a shiny red nose.

At least it matched her eyes, Tom thought, secretly; and smiled tight-lipped at his rude joke.

Elk and Gemsbok sat close together and formed a disjointed L-shape, as viewed from above. They were in precisely the same spot they'd been seen last—a small clearing near an even smaller lake. After landing and examining their cabins, it surprised no one that they contained ten and twelve stubbornly sleeping people, respectively.

Tom asked Barb and Sammy to determine if the two landers were flight-worthy; and if they weren't, to estimate what it would take to make them so. Tom then stepped outside to think.

The small lake he'd spotted from the air covered about five acres and wasn't much more than a hundred feet away. He walked down the gently sloping hill toward the water's edge.

As he progressed, he noticed details of the local plant-life he had missed earlier. The thick carpet of red grass he was walking on, for example. Its individual blades were about three inches long—typical of many varieties of genetically engineered Earth grasses. But the blades of this grass were three times wider than any he remembered seeing on Earth, or on any colony world for that matter. What's more, his original impression that the grass mimicked having been mowed, was easily seen to be wrong. The tops of the blades were not cut-off square; they were rounded, like the ends of Popsicle sticks.

Popsicle sticks! How long has it been since I've seen a wooden Popsicle stick? Eighty years? No; almost Ninety! He remembered back when he was nine or ten, making a tiny house by gluing Popsicle sticks together. He hadn't actually eaten the hundred or so Popsicles the project would have required. His mother bought a bag of them for a dollar at a yard sale. And when he'd shown her his work of art, she praised him endlessly for the creativity and cleverness he'd used in making that crummy little house. She never once pointed out that the thing was lopsided, had no windows and no floor; it didn't even have a door.

Was that why he'd married Maggie? Because she'd been just as free with praise as his mother?

As he walked, Tom realized that there were not one, but two types of trees in the forest: short bushy trees with an abundance of small round leaves, and tall majestic trees with leaves that were fewer, but heavy and broad.

The leaves of the small trees were smooth flat disks, as small as a child's palm. While the leaves of the tall trees resembled those of a maple, but were much larger—over a foot wide. Their underside was reinforced with a radiating pattern of bright yellow, thickened ribs. These yellow ribs stood out stark and bold on the huge red leaves.

As the wind blew, the leaves of the small trees fluttered against one another with a sound like distant crickets. But the larger, stiffer leaves of the tall trees rustled in the same wind like the tough dry wings of mummified bats.

Tom stopped at the water's edge and scanned its breeze-rippled surface. He'd never before stood on an earth-like planet that was devoid of animal life. He surprised himself by instinctively searching for a splash or expanding ripple that might mark the location of a fish or surface-skimming insect. He tried to stop, but his mind rebelled.

Momentarily confused, he again tried to stop—not just because such a search was a waste of time, but because it was an obvious indication that his instincts were stronger than his conscious mind. A thought repugnant to most people who think themselves civilized.

He managed to force his eyes down to the shallow water near his feet. Sunlight streamed all the way to its sandy bottom. The water was clean and smooth and fishless; populated only by bright red weeds.

Finally satisfied, his rebellious instincts gave up the search and let him scan the thick forest on the lake's far side. But his

PLAGUE AT REDHOOK

eye soon caught movement in the grass near his feet. He looked down and discovered an extra shadow next to his own. He was not alarmed. The shadow was oval.

He looked to the distant forest again. "Medsys, could these people have caught some kind of disease? Could that be what's making them sleep so long?"

The sphere levitating behind him said, "I'm having each person's medcom run a full set of tests. I'm almost done collecting the blood, serum and plasma data. After that I'll check the urine, gastric and cerebrospinal fluids. If nothing shows, I'll run tests on pancreatic and renal functions."

"Have you learned anything so far?"

"The toxicology results are in—all negative. Other than that, the preliminary results identify a couple of people with high cholesterol and one with a slightly low white-count. But that should be considered normal in a randomly mixed group like this."

"Are you saying they aren't sick? That this isn't some kind of strange alien disease?"

"I've found a number of puzzles, Captain, but nothing that would point to a cause, and certainly not a disease. At least not so far."

"What kind of puzzles?"

"For one thing, during the last sixteen days, none of the sleepers seem to have metabolized any of their muscle tissue or body fat. They weigh the same now as they did sixteen days ago."

"But that's—"

"Impossible? Yes, I know. There's more: the beards of the male sleepers do not display sixteen days worth of growth. I would guess they exhibit, at most, one day's growth. But this is trivial compared to the condition of one individual. A woman named Mary Alice Clifford has, like the others, been sleeping comfortably for these sixteen days. And, like the others, the current data from her medcom indicate that she is in good health—not perfect health, mind you, but good health."

"So?"

"She's diabetic."

"What?" Even this surprise didn't get Tom to turn around and look at the machine. "Wait a minute. How do you know that?"

"This fact is recorded in her medcom."

Tom closed his eyes and shook his head. "I still say the medcoms could be wrong."

"I was almost ready to believe that myself. However, if you check, as I did, your own ship's manifest, you will discover that Livingstone has brought one Mary Alice Clifford a package described as: Extended Insulin Zinc Suspension; six bottles; 100 units. The authorization for her to receive such a quantity of prescription medicine is also included in the manifest. It has been provided and countersigned by a doctor associated with a hospital on Earth that specializes in two diseases—one of which is diabetes."

"I know this is going to sound crazy," Tom said, "but couldn't she have ordered it to. . . I don't know, to sell on the black-market, or something?"

"It's been fifty years since insulin has been more expensive than a mixed drink. There is no black market for it. Face it, Captain: the woman is diabetic."

Tom looked up at the two clouds in the sky; they lacked the puffiness of those he'd seen earlier today; instead they stretched out long and thin. "How's her blood sugar?"

"Normal—for anyone but her. Whatever's keeping her asleep is also keeping her alive. It's the most amazing thing I've ever seen. She should have died of insulin shock twelve days ago."

"Her medcom ran out of insulin?"

"No, not at all. It's been waiting all this time for her blood sugar to drop so it could release the next dose into her bloodstream. But her blood sugar never dropped. It hasn't varied in sixteen days."

"Sixteen days. Everything is sixteen days. I'm gonna' get tired of hearing that number." He raised a hand and wiped his cheek. He glanced at the hand as he brought it down, and jerked back in such alarm that he almost stumbled backward onto the red grass. His hand was smeared with blood.

He turned around to face the machine. "Medsys?"

The medsys floated closer to examine the problem. "Do not concern yourself, Captain. The small cut you received earlier has simply been bleeding. I'll change the dressing."

"I'd like to watch."

"As you wish."

An image appeared in Tom's visual field which contained most of his own head. He saw his white hair, his green eyes, and the little white bandage the medsys had placed on his cheek—only now the bandage was saturated with blood.

"Why is it bleeding?" Tom asked.

"I closed it with a surgical adhesive; you must have inadvertently pulled it open."

"I don't remember pulling it open."

"Don't worry about it, Captain. I'll just seal it shut again. A small cut like this shouldn't be a problem."

The medsys unrolled itself; much like an armadillo or a tiny sow bug unrolling from its defensive disguise of being nothing more than an armored ball. Once open, the medsys was still only one and a half feet wide, but was nearly three feet tall. It hung motionless in the air, like an elliptical shield on the arm of an invisible warrior.

The machine's soft underbelly—a white plastic wall made lumpy by a complex assortment of sealed doors—was now fully exposed to Tom's view. Behind those doors, sterile compartments containing instruments, tools, sensors and highly specialized sets of robotic arms, remained hidden.

Eight small spotlights, encircling the medsys' belly, glared to life and swung their variable focusing beams up to Tom's cheek. Tom felt the intensity of their light converge on his skin with a distinct sensation of warmth—like concentrated sunlight.

Stephen Euin Cobb

A compartment snapped open and released a pair of thin, delicate arms, made beautiful by the glint of their gold-plating. As they worked, they flashed brightly in the light of the eight focused beams. These arms, however, were not modeled after their human counterparts; nor were their hands. The hands possessed fingers that ended in still smaller hands. And, likewise, those hands had still smaller hands available at the tips of their fingers. Tom wasn't sure how many times this was repeated, only that the medsys could perform the tiniest and most delicate microsurgery on a moment's notice.

He had a sudden flashback of the last surgical procedure he had undergone. Two years ago, he'd told the medsys that his vision was getting blurry again—thinking he just needed another radial keratotomy. But after examining his eyes, the machine told him that part of the retina inside his left eye had come loose from the back of his eyeball and had drifted a short distance forward. Re-attaching this detached retina would require surgery, so the medsys had given him a local anesthetic to numb the surface of his eye, and used a fine needle to give him an injection in the eye's far left corner.

The injection did not contain medicine, but a pure saline solution with several hundred microscopically small nanotechnological robots swimming about in it. These nano-robots were so small that if twenty of them were to form a chain by holding hands, the chain would not be able to reach around a single human hair. Once inside Tom's eyeball, the nano-robots swam and crawled to the loose area of retina, gently pulled it back into place, and re-attached it using standard laser surgical techniques.

Tom had remained conscious throughout the procedure, so the medsys had let him watch the surgery as it progressed. Several of the nano-robots provided live, if rather crude, visual feeds throughout. When they were done, the nano-robots swam back to the tiny hole through which they'd entered and crawled out onto the surface of Tom's eye. Once outside, they climbed to the tip of one of Tom's eyelashes, where the medsys was able

PLAGUE AT REDHOOK

to collect them for re-sterilization and storage; and eventually, reuse.

Tom felt a tugging on his cheek as the medsys removed the blood-soaked bandage.

"By the way, Captain. I've taken samples of the grass and trees on this planet to check their biochemistry. As far as I can determine, they pose no threat to human or machine. They contain no poisons, corrosives or known irritants."

"Good. One less thing to worry about."

Tom felt a warm, moist, rubbing sensation as the medsys cleaned his little cut. Then a cool, soothing feeling as it applied the surgical adhesive. Then a mild but insistent pinch as it carefully pressed the exposed surfaces of the cut together to seal them.

His PC said, "Tom, Barb is calling you."

"Put her through," he said, not even aware how convenient it was that he could speak without moving his mouth and disturbing the medsys' work. "Yes, Barb?"

"I've checked both Gemsbok and Elk. Neither is flight-worthy. They both have the same problem Caribou has: somebody took a hammer to their electric generators. I can fix them, but only with spare parts from Gazelle's hangar deck."

"I was afraid of that," Tom said. "I'm not too keen on leaving sleepers down here unattended, even for a short time." He paused for a second. "Maybe we should just pile them all into Zebra and take them up to Gazelle in one move. Then we could wait for the emergency team from—"

"Tom!" Sammy yelled. "Come quick! It's that woman again! She's inside Zebra!"

The medsys withdrew its golden arms from Tom's face and stowed them back inside its belly. Tom headed for Zebra at what, considering his age, might best be regarded as a dead run. Even so, the medsys—once again curled into a ball—breezed passed him before he was halfway there.

As Tom reached Zebra's side door, he heard a woman near the craft's tail scream with her mouth. Realizing she must be outside the lab's rear loading door, he ran around to the back. But when he got there, all he saw was Sammy with a tool in his hand, breathing hard and looking angry.

"She got away!" Sammy shook the tool as though threatening the nearby forest. "And I nearly had her too!"

"Did she hurt you?"

"No, she ran the moment she saw me."

"Do you have any idea what she wanted?"

"I think she came to smash the generators, like on the other landers."

"Did she?"

"No, I was inspecting them when I heard a noise down the hall that sounded like someone hammering. When I went to look, I saw her laying on her stomach on the dining room floor. Her arms and head were down in the hyperlight drive's access hatch. She was smashing the drive gimbals!"

"What? Did she do much damage?"

"She did enough," Sammy said, bitterly. "It's not leaving the ground."

Tom glanced at Zebra, then looked back at Sammy. "Can you and Barb fix it?"

"Sure, if you don't mind us taking the gimbals off Elk or Gemsbok."

"How long will that take?"

"About eighteen hours. More, if we run into problems."

"Then we're stuck here for the night?"

"Yep. Looks like it."

The medsys floated out through the lab's rear door, followed by Barb, and joined the two men. Tom noticed without comment; instead, he looked up at the long thin strips of cloud in the beautiful blue sky. Those on his left had changed from white to a pale shade of pink. The sun was getting low. Sunset was beginning.

"Wait a minute." Tom scowled. "How did she get here so fast? We're twenty-one miles from Caribou and we saw her there less than two hours ago."

Sammy shrugged. "Maybe she ran."

"She would have had to run the whole way, at full speed, without stopping to rest!"

"Maybe she's a long distance runner," Sammy suggested, but without much enthusiasm.

Tom didn't look convinced. "PC, get me Gazelle."

"This is Gazelle."

"The mad-woman. . . Umm. . . Doctor Sharon Rice—is she a long distance runner?"

"No, Captain. Quite the contrary. During the four years that she's been a member of this survey team, she's led an entirely sedentary lifestyle. She's had to; she suffers from chronic asthma."

Chapter 9

Rude Arrival

Mark spent an hour trying to learn what happened from the passionate-woman, but no matter what her sedation level, her mind remained squarely on sex and nothing else. The only thing he was able to get out of her was that everything was fine until the day after an old man with bushy gray hair came aboard. A scientist named Wilson or Williams.

Her PC refused to divulge where she was or what she was doing when the explosion occurred. Mark had run into this kind of information-wall many times before with other patients. All PCs had this option programmed into them. Exercising it usually indicated the owner had been doing something highly personal at the moment in question. Mark was willing to bet this patient had been engaged in some kind of sexual activity.

Mark made the rounds of the undead; examining each and reviewing their individual medical records as accumulated by their medcoms. Most of their PCs still functioned, but seemed to know little about what had caused the explosion. He took three full sets of tissue samples and prepared them for multiple

PLAGUE AT REDHOOK

laboratory analysis. One set of samples to be analyzed here aboard Pasteur, the others he would send by torpedo to laboratories on Earth and Big Sandy.

During all this, paramedic number one had stayed with the hand and monitored its progress. "Launch torpedoes," Mark said to Pasteur's comsys as he approached the hand's cage. His voice changed slightly. "How is it doing?"

"Its wrist is two millimeters longer," number one said.

"So it's true. It really is growing an arm."

"Yes."

Somehow, with all its other magic tricks, Mark was not shocked by this final coup. But even this begged one more question. "When will it stop?"

"What?"

"When will it stop growing?"

"I don't understand," said one.

"Will it grow only an arm? Or will it grow a shoulder? A chest? A head?"

The paramedic didn't answer at first. Then it said, "I think we'll have to wait and see."

"Doctor!" said Pasteur's comsys, "we are surrounded by military assault robots."

"What!?"

"You are being paged by a military commander."

"Put him through."

"It is a woman."

"Oh."

A face appeared in his mind: a middle aged woman with hair as black as his own, but with bright gray streaks at both temples. Her hair was combed straight back, and long enough that it hung down behind her shoulders. Her shirt collar was a stiff military style; thick, black, formal. It occurred to Mark that it was probably artificial wool, and probably designed specifically to appear uncomfortable. She glared at him as though angry about something terribly important.

Mark tried to sound cordial. "Commander, this is an unexpected—

"What do those two torpedoes contain?" she demanded without bothering to introduce herself.

Mark was doubly shocked. First, by what she'd said, and then again because her mouth had moved in perfect time with every word. He stumbled mentally. "What?"

"You launched two message torpedoes," she said, harshly; clearly speaking with her mouth. "What do they contain?"

"Tissue samples and descriptions of the patients we recovered from the Star Shuttle Andromeda."

"Where are they going?" she demanded.

"To Community Hospital on Big Sandy and to Mount Sinai Hospital on Earth."

The commander glanced at someone off screen. "Intercept."

"Aye, aye" came the disembodied response.

She faced Mark again. "Doctor, you and your ship, as well as the shuttle Andromeda, are hereby placed under quarantine of the highest level: Class one—Plague. I repeat: Class one—Plague. If you fail to follow my instructions at any time, I can—if I chose—use lethal force. I can, with a single command, and without any possible legal reprisal by your family or other legal heirs, destroy you and your ship. Do you understand?"

Half of the commander's face—along with half of her long black hair and one gray streak—was momentarily bleached white, as a nearby screen displayed the blinding flash of one, and then another, distant nuclear explosion. Mark's two communication torpedoes, and their tissue-sample cargoes, had ceased to exist.

Mark's mouth hung open, though no sound escaped.

"Answer me! Do you understand?"

Chapter 10

Symptoms of Confusion

Since Zebra was not yet leaving the planet's surface, Tom decided to let most of the sleepers stay where they were for the night and simply lock their landers with fresh encryption codes. However, before securing Elk and Gemsbok Tom instructed Sammy, Barb and the medsys to move six of Zebra's sleepers out of their bunks, and lay them upon blankets spread on Elk's dining room floor. When this little operation was complete, Tom and his crew all had proper sleeping quarters. Tom and Blair each had a small private room, and Sammy and Barb had one they could share.

With his crew provided for, and Elk and Gemsbok secure, Tom said his good nights, closed his door, removed most of his clothing and climbed into the lower bunk. He'd now been awake for thirty-two hours, and while he didn't actually feel tired yet—what with all the excitement—he felt sure he would fall asleep easily as soon as he stretched out in a comfortable bunk.

He could not possibly have been more wrong. He tossed. He turned. He got up and fixed himself a glass of warm milk. After drinking it and returning to bed, he still didn't feel tired.

Perhaps some music, he thought.

He pictured in his mind a stereo console. Then imagined pulling an antique plastic disk—the kind once called a *CD*—from a stack of similar disks.

He wasn't actually old enough to have bought a CD in his youth—they'd faded out of existence just before he was ten. He wasn't even old enough to remember that CD stood for *Compact Disk*. But they'd been so popular for so long, that decades before he'd been born they were well entrenched as the universal computer icon representing Music. Imagining one was certainly easy enough, he'd seen hundreds in old movies.

He read its imaginary label—already having decided what words that label would bear. It was Beethoven's ninth symphony.

He slid the disk into a slot on the nonexistent console's face, and relaxing music filled his mind. It was too loud for sleeping, so he imagined reaching a hand out and turning the console's volume knob counterclockwise. The music softened in perfect accord with the imagined rotation. He didn't bother checking the visual display of the music's wave form and frequency patterns, but he did soften the bass by pulling down a few of the sliders on the console's graphic equalizer.

After twenty minutes of listening to soothing music—while staring open-eyed into the darkness—he decided to give up trying to force himself into sleep. He would just read a book instead. "PC," he said, "download a novel from Livingstone's library for me."

He could have envisioned a shelf of books and simply plucked out the one with the desired title. But he wasn't quite sure what he wanted.

"What would you like?"

"A mystery, I think. We're definitely faced with one here."

"Do you have a title in mind? Or an author?"

"Agatha Christie."

"You've read all her mysteries. Would you like to re-read one?"

"No. How about Arthur Conan Doyle? One of his Sherlock Holmes stories."

"There is only one you have not read: The Sign of Four. It's one of his longer works."

"Good. Maybe it'll inspire me to use some deductive reasoning on our situation here. That, or put me to sleep."

"As you wish. Would you like me to read it to you?"

"No. My eyes aren't tired yet."

"Several motion picture versions have been made. Some of them, quite good. Would you like to watch this story rather than read it?"

"No. I'm hoping reading will make me sleepy."

"Very well."

The title page of the requested novel appeared in the center of Tom's field of vision. The words looked as though printed with high quality black ink on a single sheet of white paper measuring a foot and a half wide and two feet tall. Oddly, it also looked as though the page was suspended, not in the air, as was usual, but well inside the bed directly above him.

He imagined turning the page.

The title page disappeared and was replaced with the first page of the story. Tom began reading. Two hours later he'd finished and still wasn't the least bit sleepy. He downloaded an old movie and laid in bed watching that. When it was over he watched another, and then another.

During all this time, the cut on his cheek provided him with a tiny, but sharp, pain. Tiny enough to be ignored for long stretches of time, but eventually its persistence won out. He finally succumbed to the temptation of rubbing it, and once again found his hand smeared with blood.

"Medsys, are you monitoring?"

"Yes, Captain."

"Would you mind putting a new bandage on this thing? That surgical adhesive just isn't working."

"Strange. I've never had a problem with it before. I'll be there within five minutes."

Tom got out of bed, pulled on his clothes and went out into the hall. The sun was up. It filled the dining room with as much morning light as could be squeezed through the little round windows. He stepped into one of Zebra's two bathrooms and looked in the mirror to see the bandage on his cheek. It was soaked with blood.

But something else was wrong too. Something about his face. Something he couldn't quite put a finger on. He squinted and turned his head slowly from side to side to examine it from different angles; trying to figure out what it might be.

Then he got it.

He leaned closer to the mirror and rubbed his chin with his hand. His face was as smooth as a baby's butt. There were no whiskers on his chin, or his cheeks, or his neck. His beard had not grown at all during the night. He thought of the sleeper's beards. His eyes grew wide and he felt a cold chill crawl up his back. None of the males had needed a shave!

"Medsys!"

"Medsys here. What's all the excitement?"

"I've caught it! Whatever's affected the sleepers; I've got it too!"

"Calm down. I'm on my way. Do you feel tired? Like you might fall asleep?"

"No. I haven't been able to sleep all night."

"Then what makes you think you've caught what they've got?" The medsys floated into the bathroom and stopped next to Tom's shoulder.

"Look!" Tom rubbed his face to emphasize the lack of whiskers. "My beard's stopped growing!"

"I see," the machine said slowly, as though pondering this new fact. But then resumed normal conversational speed with: "That's not a good sign. How do you feel?"

PLAGUE AT REDHOOK

"Fine."

"Any weakness, nausea, dizziness, headache? Pain of any sort? Anywhere in you body?"

"No," Tom said weakly, openly confused by the sudden barrage of questions. He looked down at his body as if expecting to find the answers written on his shirt. He looked back at the medsys; surprised at the truth. "No, I feel fine."

"Your medcom seems to agree. It finds nothing unusual in your measurements. But didn't you say you haven't slept all night?"

"Yeah."

"How do you usually sleep? Have you ever had problems falling asleep before?"

"No. Not in the last decade. I had a few rough years after Maggie died, but that was eighteen years ago. Other than that, I've slept fine."

"Are you sure?"

Tom knew what the medsys meant. And yes, it had begun to play on his nerves. He'd begun worrying about his upcoming death more than a year ago. It seemed to tower in front of him like an angry giant, waiting only for the appropriate moment to squash him flat and grind him into oblivion.

And it was unavoidable. In about seventeen years, Tom's health would begin to fail; two or three years after that and he would be dead. He knew this to be true. Everybody did. And why not? This was the way most everyone's life ended nowadays. Unless you were killed in some kind of terrible accident, modern medical science kept you relatively strong, and relatively healthy, until about the age of 115. At which point, all the cells in your body—with a stubbornness that seemed to laugh in the face of medical science—stopped reproducing. With no new cells to replace those constantly expiring, your entire body deteriorated swiftly. At the end of a couple of very ugly years, you died.

And since it was unavoidable, there was nothing to do but either ignore it, or worry about it. Tom generally tried to put on a jovial front, but he suspected the medsys had already pegged him as a worrier. Even so, his answer was more true than false.

"Yes, I'm sure. I've been sleeping fine."

"This is interesting. Your sleeplessness, I mean. I've just spent the night sitting up with Blair. She couldn't sleep either. Originally I'd blamed this on her flu, but now I wonder if she hasn't been affected also. Pardon, one moment. I have an idea."

The medsys fell silent. Tom took another look at himself in the mirror.

The voice of the medsys returned. "I've just re-examined the data I downloaded from the medcoms of Dr. Sharon Rice and Dr. Stanley Brewer during our original, albeit brief, encounter. I wasn't fortunate enough at the time to get a full set of data covering the last sixteen days, but the nine days of data I did get was enough to confirm my theory."

"What theory?"

"During the last nine days, and probably longer, neither of them has slept."

"Not at all?"

"That is correct. I think you can consider this good news. It suggests you will not be joining the sleepers."

"I'd rather sleep than go insane."

"Only one of these two people seems to be insane. The other appears normal."

"Normal?" Tom's head bobbed up and down. "The man was so consumed with panic, he talked through his mouth! You call that sane?" Tom cringed with disgust, remembering how the long wet string of mucus felt as it stuck to his arms.

"Wouldn't you be frightened, Captain, if someone were trying to kill you? Such behavior strikes me as well within the bounds of normalcy."

"Wait a minute. Aren't you the one that told me the man's PC claimed he would be scared with or without her?"

"True. But the opinion of the man's PC concerning his emotional state has yet to be supported by any other evidence."

PLAGUE AT REDHOOK

Tom shook his head. "I don't know; his fear looked mighty—"

Tom's PC said, "Sorry to interrupt, but Sammy's calling you, and he sounds upset."

"Put him through. Yes, Sammy?"

"Tom!" Sammy yelled. "Something's wrong with Barb!"

"Is she hurt?"

"Yes! No! I mean. She can't stop laughing!"

"What?"

"She's been laughing for ten minutes. She can't stop!"

The medsys broke in. "How did this start?"

"We were removing the gimbals from Gemsbok's drive; telling jokes and laughing—everything was fine. But then she laughed at a joke and didn't stop. After two or three minutes I got worried, so I pinched her arm. But she still didn't stop; so I slapped her face. Normally, that would have made her mad enough to slap me right back, but it didn't even slow her down."

"Why were you two working at this hour?" asked the medsys. "Have you been up all night?"

"Yeah, but that's not important." The fear displayed in Sammy's words rose steadily. "We've got to do something! She's laughing so hard she might hurt herself! She might hurt the baby! Tom, I'm getting scared!"

Things were getting too bizarre. Tom no longer even knew what to say. It didn't matter; the medsys didn't give him a chance. "First of all, you've got to calm down," it said. "Try and keep her comfortable. We'll be there in ninety seconds."

The medsys breezed out of the bathroom, exited Zebra, and headed for Gemsbok through the damp morning air—with Tom jogging along close behind. They found Sammy crying in Gemsbok's dining room, and Barb laughing in the hall.

Tom was not surprised to see Sammy crying. These crazy symptoms were enough to make anyone scared. He also knew Sammy had a special reason to worry. Vigorous physical movement might be all right for most pregnant women, but this couple had been avoiding anything that even looked like it might hurt their baby. The extra caution was justified; their only previous child had been stillborn.

"Captain," the medsys said, "You might try to comfort Sammy, while I see what I can do for Barb."

"Good idea."

Over the years, Tom had accumulated an abundance of experience in comforting people. It wasn't that he had witnessed any more suffering, pain or death per decade than others; only that he'd been witnessing it for nearly a century.

He walked over to Sammy and put an arm around his shoulder. He didn't have any brilliant words with which to cheer him, so he just squeezed him gently. For some unknown reason many people find comfort in being squeezed. Tom figured Sammy might be one of them. He must have been right; Sammy didn't stop crying, but at least he cried a little more quietly.

Tom looked over at the medsys. Barb was laughing at it.

Her laughter was that of the true and ancient tradition. Driven by contractions of the diaphragm, it exited her mouth as great bursts of air.

She covered her mouth with both hands and closed her eyes, as if trying to hold it in. This worked for a few seconds, but when she opened her eyes and looked at the medsys again, she laughed right in its so-to-speak face.

"Barb?" it said.

Between convulsive belly laughs, she managed to think, "I'm sorry!"

She put her hand on the wall to brace herself. She was laughing so hard Tom thought for sure she would collapse to the floor. It even occurred to him that without the thought-link she wouldn't be able to communicate at all.

"Are you laughing at me?" asked the medsys.

"No!" She bent over and directed her laughter at the floor. "I'm sorry. Everything is just so funny!"

"Are you in any pain?"

"My stomach muscles hurt. But only when I laugh!" She noticed Tom, and screamed with delight. "Tom! You wouldn't believe how funny you look right now." And with that she laughed even louder than before.

The medsys asked, "Are you laughing at Tom?"

"Yes, he's so funny!"

"What is it about him that makes him funny?"

"I don't know. He just is!" She looked up at the ceiling. "I know I'm being rude," she said, laughing over every word, "but I can't help it!"

"Are you sure you are unable to stop?"

"Yes. I've tried, and tried."

"Then I'm going to have your medcom give you a sedative. Do you understand what I'm saying? You will begin to feel sleepy. Do you understand?"

"Yes!"

Within seconds her laughter softened and her body started to relax. Tom left Sammy to guide her across the room into a comfortable easy chair.

Once she was dozing quietly, Tom and the medsys sat Sammy down and asked him a few questions. Sammy, however, had trouble concentrating. He was still crying.

Without the thought-link, Sammy too might have been unable to communicate. Even so, the imaginary voice that he projected through the link sounded frighteningly high in pitch and tightly stressed. "There wasn't anything unusual," he said, as he wiped tears from both cheeks. "Everything was fine until she couldn't stop laughing."

"Didn't you say you hadn't slept?" asked the medsys.

"Well. . . yeah."

"Why not?"

Sammy's bawling softened to a steady whimper—perhaps due to the strain of recalling events from his short-term memory. "When Tom went to bed, we weren't tired yet. So we figured we'd put in a couple of hours pulling Gemsbok's gimbals. We don't usually sleep as much as Tom anyway. What's the big deal?"

"But you stayed up all night."

"We didn't feel tired, so we just kept working." He wiped his face again. "What's wrong with that?"

The medsys explained exactly what was wrong with it. Then asked, "Do you feel tired now?"

"No. Not a bit." Sammy interrupted his crying long enough to sniffle loudly several times in a row. His nose was filled with tears. "Now that you mention it, I'm not hungry either—and I should be. I haven't eaten anything since yesterday evening."

"I haven't eaten," Tom said, "but I'm starved."

"Hunger," the medsys said, "or the lack of it, may or may not be a symptom. Captain, as an experiment, I would like you to eat a full meal."

"OK, but let me step into the washroom first. I need to pee."

"As you wish. In the interim, I'll review Sammy and Barb's medcom data covering the last few hours."

Tom left to attend to his personal business, but soon returned looking worried.

"Is something wrong?" asked the medsys.

Tom didn't respond.

"Did you urinate?"

"Yes."

"Was there a problem? Pain? Discomfort?"

Tom shook his head. "No pain." But his tone sounded confused—even to himself.

"Then what's wrong?"

"I feel like I still need to go."

"Did you empty your bladder completely?"

"Yes."

"Are you sure?"

"Yeah. I mean, I do know how to pee!"

"Do you feel as though you need to urinate just as strongly now, as you did before?"

"Yes."

"Then this may be a symptom too. Now I am even more interested in seeing the results of your eating. The question is, will you continue to feel hungry even though your stomach is full?"

Tom turned and stared wild-eyed at Sammy. Tom's facial expression had changed from confusion to that of a man suddenly terrified by impending doom. He lunged at Sammy, grabbed him by the shoulders and shook him hard. "Sammy! Stop crying! Stop crying right now!"

But Sammy's crying only grew louder. He looked up at Tom with teardrops clinging to every eyelash. "Is Barb going to die? Are we going to lose the baby?"

"Sammy, you've got to stop crying!" Tom shook him again. "We can't afford for you to get stuck like this!"

"Captain, please calm down," the medsys said. "We can't afford for you to become stuck in an emotional extreme either."

Tom took a quick step backward, then closed his eyes and put his hands up—surrender fashion—to signify he was making a determined effort. Once he'd composed himself, he put his hands down and said, "I'm all right."

Tom's PC said, "Tom, the medsys has called me on one of the low-level data channels. It is requesting that you continue your conversation on a secure channel."

"So Sammy and Barb won't hear?"

"Presumably. And it wants it scrambled."

"OK; do what it says."

"Very well. Switching audio-thought-link from channel twelve to channel 143. Engaging numerical scramble code. . . Now."

"OK, medsys," Tom said. "What's the big secret?"

"No secret. I just wanted you to feel free to discuss Sammy and Barb's medical conditions without fear of damaging their morale."

"Oh. Still, there must be something you wanted to say."

"True. Sammy and Barb's conditions may explain the behavior of the mad-woman and the frightened-man. It's possible that, like Sammy and Barb, they were each experiencing their respective emotions, and then simply became stuck with them. The question is, what could cause emotional states to get locked into place?"

"Yeah, and how long will they stay locked?" added Tom.

"Sharon Rice and Stanley Brewer have had their symptoms for sixteen days. We must face the prospect that whatever state gets locked-in may remain indefinitely."

"You mean permanent?"

"Perhaps."

Tom looked at Sammy. The poor man sat hunched in his chair, his hands covering his face. Tears ran between his fingers and dripped onto the carpet. The way he moaned and wailed you'd think the baby was already dead.

Tom looked at Barb: sprawled in the easy chair; loose, relaxed, comfortable; her limbs jutted and folded every-which-way, and her nine and a half months worth of pregnant belly pointing straight up at the ceiling. Her breathing seemed a bit fast, and perhaps a bit shallow, but that was probably just due to the sedative.

He looked at the medsys. "Is there still no evidence that this is some kind of disease?"

"Nothing concrete. At least not yet. I've had everyone's medcom look and re-look for evidence of germs, bacteria, viruses. None have been detected, even in the sleepers, and they've been exposed to this biosphere far longer than we have. However, I should stress that the medcoms have only been searching for chemical byproducts of an infectious agent, not for the agent itself. So these results do not prove there isn't one; just that if there is, it can't be detected by these methods."

"Then let me rephrase the question. Do you personally believe this is being caused by a microorganism?"

PLAGUE AT REDHOOK

"Yes. If for not other reason than it seems to have affected every human being, but not so much as one artificially intelligent machine. I've run every possible systems check on myself, Zebra's comsys, and all the PCs in the sleepers and in your crew, and I have yet to find even the slightest deviation from normalcy. Granted, the comsyses aboard Caribou, Gemsbok and Elk are unconscious, but that's only because they have no electrical power."

"That's all I need," Tom said. "PC, I'm about to make a general announcement. See to it that it reaches everyone in this star system, both human and machine, with two exceptions: Sharon Rice and Stanley Brewer."

Still crying, Sammy looked up at Tom, but said nothing.

"I have paged all the parties you requested," Tom's PC said. "Those that are conscious have acknowledged that you have their attention. You may proceed when ready."

"Thank you." Tom paused for a moment to decide where to begin. "This is a general announcement," he said. "As the only officer in this star system who is still functional, I am placing this planet: E-33, including its entire biosphere, under medical quarantine. The aforementioned zone will remain off-limits to all outside parties, human or machine, until we learn what is causing these strange symptoms. I hereby assign Gazelle the duty of alerting outsiders—should any enter this star system—to the dangers of this quarantine. As soon as the lander Zebra is flight-worthy, assuming my crew is in any condition to make it flight-worthy, we will transport all humans, including those currently sleeping, but not including Sharon Rice or Stanley Brewer, off the planet and up to the survey ship Gazelle; which will then *also* become quarantined. Once aboard Gazelle, we will wait for the arrival of the U.N. emergency team, who will then have the authority to continue or discontinue this quarantine. I will also leave it to them to decide what to do about Sharon Rice and Stanley Brewer. This ends the general announcement."

Tom's PC said, "Gazelle is calling."

"Put it through. Yes, Gazelle?"

"Captain. Considering the turn of events, and especially your declaration of a state of quarantine, I must inform you that there is one person who should, by all the rules governing quarantine, be included in this, but who is not."

"What are you talking about? Who did I leave out?"

"Doctor Aaron Williams, an exo-biochemist. He had been part of our survey team for just over two years, but after his 80th birthday he left us to take a rather prestigious research post in his home town. Before he left, he spent two days gathering and analyzing biological specimens on the surface of E-33."

"He was here? Where is he now?"

"Aboard the Star Shuttle, Andromeda."

"Have any other ships besides Andromeda made physical contact with this planet, or with the survey team after they'd been to this planet's surface?"

"No."

"What about other types of physical contact? Have you sent out any communication torpedoes?"

"No, Captain. Not since we arrived at this planet. You sent two, but that was before you'd made physical contact either with the planet, or with me."

"Then the only escaped carrier of this mystery disease—if it is a disease—is this Doctor Williams?"

"Correct."

"How long ago did he leave?"

"Seventeen days."

"And where would he be now?"

"Still aboard the Star Shuttle Andromeda, on his way home. It's a long trip."

"Where is his home?"

"New York City."

Chapter 11

Jumping Spiders

Mark placed a tissue sample into a small stainless-steel frame, then carefully slid the frame into the side of a complicated looking appliance: a portable electron microscope. He closed its airtight hatch, sealing the frame and tissue sample inside the microscope's tiny airlock—the entry way to its vacuum chamber.

In vacuum, the sample would be bombarded with a finely focused beam of electrons. Only in vacuum could a beam of electrons be artfully manipulated by magnetic fields in such a way as to produce a vastly magnified image of the sample.

As the machine chugged softly, pumping air from its airlock, Mark was forced to exercise patience.

The instrument's standard controls and display screen were mounted on the unit's front. Mark ignored these.

Through the link, by way of his PC, he contacted the microscope's internal computer, and informed it that he wished to receive all images directly into his mind. The microscope immediately furnished him with an imaginary control panel for display inside the visual portion of his brain.

The chugging stopped. Vacuum had been achieved.

Mark adjusted the imaginary controls and felt a sensation of coldness spread over most of his back while he stared intently at the images thus produced. The coldness was simply the evaporation of unneeded sweat. "What do you make of it?" he asked number one, without first verifying that the paramedic floating next to him was viewing these same images. It was.

"I'm... I'm not sure." The paramedic sounded stumped—a fact that did not make Mark feel better about his own confusion. Quite the contrary; it filled him with an unfamiliar sense of dread. "I've never seen anything like it," the machine said. "Never."

Mark tried to be analytical, or at least associative. "It looks a little bit like the inside of a bee hive; except that the hive cells aren't hexagonal, and the bees—if I can call them that for the moment. The bees aren't so crowded together as they usually are in a bee hive, and they're far smaller than the cells. And, having no wings, the bees actually look more like chubby ants. Or..." Mark hesitated at the somewhat repulsive thought. "Or jumping spiders. That's it," he decided, "they look just like jumping spiders."

"Yes, they do resemble jumping spiders," said one. "But clearly, they are not spiders."

"Agreed. At two microns in length, they're too small to be organisms of such complexity. Which means they can't be living things. They must be some kind of nanotechnology. Some kind of nano-robots."

"And that hive...", said the machine. "It seems to be a series of artificial cells. Cells that look and feel and act like living tissue, but which in fact are not alive at all."

"Also agreed." Mark glanced at the hand, still caged, on the examination table to his right. "So the thing isn't really alive."

"Its wrist area isn't alive. We haven't taken samples from other locations."

"I've got a bad feeling the entire hand is composed of those artificial cells. Just them, and nothing else. The nano-robots must have been building it all along; stealing raw materials from whatever was readily available. Maybe whatever it was touching: tables, floors, the cage we put it in. Hell, maybe even the dust floating by in the air."

"You may be correct. I'll sedate it and take tissue samples from various locations for confirmation: skin, blood, muscle, ligament."

"Yeah. Good." Mark nodded absently, already lost in a whirl of untransmitted stray thoughts. *I wonder who made these nano-robots. They look awfully advanced. Certainly more advanced than surgical nano-robots. Or at least those I've seen. Could they be military? The military's always had the most advanced nano-tech.*

"Shall I take a bone sample?" asked the paramedic.

Mark didn't answer. He just looked off into an imagined distance with a puzzled look on his face.

"Doctor? Shall I take a—"

"Why would it. . ." Mark thought softly. But his sentence trailed off, incomplete.

"Why would it what?" asked the machine.

Mark frowned deeply, still staring off into the distance. "Why would it bear Doctor Williams' fingerprints?"

Chapter 12

Knife Wound

Tom paced back and forth the full length of Zebra's little dining room, all the while looking down at its short-cropped blue carpet.

"I don't think he is capable of doing it," replied the medsys, which was not actually in the room with Tom a the moment. Nor was it anywhere else aboard Zebra. It was inspecting the sleepers aboard Gemsbok.

Tom shook his head without looking up. "We need him to try."

"Agreed, but in his emotional state—"

Tom stopped in his tracks. "Look, I know Sammy may not be able to handle it. But our only other choice is for *me* to do it; and I for one refuse to travel in any spacecraft repaired by *me*."

The medsys fell silent; perhaps unsure how to respond to such a blanket assertion. Finally, it said, "I'll take him off the sedation. But only so long as he appears to be making some reasonable level of progress."

Tom nodded briskly. "OK."

The machine added, "And I want you there to assist him."

Tom raised an eyebrow. "Why?"

"Because even if his mind is clear enough for the work, his hands will not be steady. The sedatives will have weakened him."

"OK, OK. I don't mind helping. As long as we get off this crazy planet." Tom dropped himself into one of the white easy chairs and closed his eyes to rest his overstressed brain for a minute or two.

Blair walked briskly into the room and came up behind him with a steak knife gripped tightly in her fist. She stopped in mid-stride, made a terrible face, then doubled over with a loud sneeze. Her twenty four hour flu was now deep into its second week.

Tom swiveled his chair around to face her.

Once she'd recovered from the sneeze she took two more steps forward and said, "Tom, you've got to see this." She placed the cutting edge of the knife against the back of her hand and pulled it from left to right across her skin. The flesh parted, and the gap began to fill with blood.

Tom jumped to his feet. "What are you doing? Are you crazy?"

Blair shook her head, rapidly. "No. Just look at it." And she held the wound out for him to see more clearly. Her hand trembled.

"Medsys, get in here!" Tom yelled through the link. "Blair's hurt!"

The medsys announced that it was on its way, but Tom wasn't listening. In his excitement he also missed the machine's request for him to send it images with which to begin a diagnosis.

The trembling of Blair's hand grew to include most of her arm. And just as the blood was about to overflow the wound and race down her fingers, all of it—every potential drop—was sucked back inside her body, and the gap closed from left to right at the same speed it had been made.

"What?!" Tom grabbed Blair's hand and stretched the skin this way and that in a vain effort to re-open the cut. But the wound wasn't just invisible, it was gone. It had closed itself, sealed itself, and left no mark.

In his amazement, Tom's lips formed the words, and he almost gave breath to them. Almost asked them out loud. "How did you do that?"

Blair yanked her hand back. "I didn't do it!"

"But! Then how did you know it would. . . ?"

She looked at her hand. "I cut myself by accident a few minutes ago and the thing healed before I could even stop swearing."

"Doesn't it hurt?"

"Well, of course it hurts!" she snapped. "Just like any other cut. Right up until the second it disappears. Then nothing. No pain at all. It's as though the cut never existed."

Tom reached out and examined her shaking hand again, then looked at his own hands.

The medsys flew in through the open door so rapidly that Tom actually considered scolding it for apparent recklessness. "What is the nature of the injury?" it demanded.

Tom looked at her. "Blair?"

She shook her head. The motion caused her trembling to grow and spread until it included her entire body. She collapsed into a nearby chair. "I don't think I can do it again. All this weirdness is getting to me. I'm sorry, Tom; if you want the medsys to see it, you'll have to demonstrate on yourself." She leaned forward and set the knife on the table, then dropped back into the seat again, limp and exhausted.

Tom looked at the knife thoughtfully for several seconds, then slowly bent down to pick it up.

"Wait!" Blair said, as she struggled back to her feet. "Wait, just a few damn seconds." And she hurried straight out the door.

Chapter 13

Rat-Tool

As Tom watched Sammy working, he couldn't help feeling pity for the poor man. Sammy toiled diligently, though sobbing and moaning incoherently every minute. He even groaned pathetically as he did the few heavy tasks. He actually seemed hunched over, as though collapsed from within. All of this was totally uncharacteristic of the Sammy Radford that Tom was familiar with.

The medsys rested its levitators by placing its spherical self in one of Zebra's dining room easy chairs. Tom avoided looking at it, as if fearing it might say, I told you so.

Sammy unbolted the access hatch in the floor of Zebra's dining room, lifted and slid it out of the way, then scrambled down head-first into the hole. As he opened the drive housing, Tom asked for and received permission to watch the action through Sammy's eyes. Such permission—by tradition and by law—can only be granted by the person through whose eyes the viewing is to be done.

Stephen Buin Cobb

The lander's drive was contained in a spherical housing of foamed-metal which was gimbal-mounted inside an aluminum ring, which was in turn gimbal-mounted inside a stainless steel frame. The double gimbals allowed the sphere to be rotated freely in any direction. Stepping motors, mounted at the gimbal points, controlled both rotations.

Tom eased himself down and sat cross-legged on the floor beside the access hatch. He was beginning to see that this was going to become another one of life's little object lessons. This lesson concerned just how much more time and trouble it takes to fix things than to destroy them. Sammy's feet and knees wiggled up through the hole.

Tom noticed Sammy pull a rat out of his tool belt. It wasn't really a rat; didn't even look like a rat; if anything it resembled a cleaning robot. But rat was what mechanics everywhere called them.

Sammy flipped the rat's power switch on and turned it loose in the crawl space under Zebra's dining room floor. He then changed his view to one as seen through the rat's eyes, and directed his little worker down into the cramped quarters in the heart of the drive, over and under and around obstacles that Sammy would never have been able to pass in person.

Tom knew Sammy was telling it what to do by pretending that he was the rat, that his body was the rat's body, and that the rat's sense of touch was his own.

One of Sammy's hands popped up through the opening and tossed aside a smashed object that Tom—who was no mechanic—was willing to guess might have been a bearing. The hand opened, and Sammy said, "Tom, hand me a fluid bearing."

Tom pointed at an object and sent his own view through the link. "You mean this?"

"No. It'll look like. . ." and from his memory, Sammy sent Tom an image of a flat cylinder.

Tom looked at an object wrapped in silvery plastic leaning against a yellow tool box. "Could that be it?"

PLAGUE AT REDHOOK

"Yeah, that's it."

Tom picked it up and placed it in Sammy's hand, which then disappeared down the hole.

"Thanks."

Tom's PC broke-in. "Tom, there is a military commander paging you."

"A what?" he said with some surprise.

"She says she is here to enforce the quarantine."

"Put her through." Tom squared his shoulders—not because she was going to see him, she wasn't. Etiquette does not require sending images of oneself to a total stranger. He squared them only to bolster his moral: something he felt a great need of at the moment. "This is Captain Thomas Vickery, of the U.N. Supply Ship Livingstone."

"Good afternoon, Captain," said a disembodied voice, in a crisp, but otherwise friendly tone. "This is Commander Dorothy Ponder of the U.N. Warship Bonaparte. I understand you are having a number of problems down there."

"Yes. Yes, we are." Tom almost laughed at the understatement.

"I have been sent to enforce the quarantine you declared. It may hearten you to learn that I've brought with me a human doctor and his U.N. hospital ship. It is my hope that he will find a way to expedite an end to this quarantine. In the meantime, my orders are that you must keep all your people on the planet's surface."

"It was my intention," said Tom, "to move everyone up to the orbiting ship, Gazelle, for the duration of the quarantine."

"I'm sorry, but that is out of the question. No one is to leave the planet's surface."

"No one?"

"No one. Under penalty of death."

Chapter 14

Fire

"I tell you, the commander will never allow it," Pasteur's comsys said. "The rules of quarantine are specific, and I can assure you she will not break them."

"But I must go to the surface," said Mark. "I must examine the symptoms of the patients on the surface first-hand. I must learn as much as possible, as quickly as possible. Lives may be at stake."

"She will refuse."

"Even so, I have to ask. Call her for me."

"As you wish."

Mark sat-up a little straighter on his lab stool and stretched his back muscles. He turned away from the microscope, slid a few tissue samples out of the way, and folded his arms on the imitation black marble lab bench. He leaned forward and let his weight rest on his arms. The surface pressing against his skin felt just cool enough to be pleasant. He considered placing his head on his folded arms but decided he wasn't quite that tired.

Suddenly, and with no clear provocation, his mind jumped back to something he'd said earlier: "I'm a married man!"

"Are you speaking to me?" asked his PC.

Mark blushed. "Huh? No, no. Just thinking out loud."

"Very well."

Mark was shocked at himself. Shocked that he'd blurted out such a non-fact to the naked-woman, and shocked that he'd done it without even recognizing it as an untruth.

He hadn't actually lied. Or at least he hadn't meant to lie. It was just that even now, after three years, he still had trouble remembering he was divorced.

He and his wife had met, fell in love, and married, all while in medical school at UCLA. After their residencies, they'd been offered positions at hospitals in different cities: He in San Francisco and she in Las Vegas. Positions much too good to pass up. They were both certain their marriage could handle this little separation; certain that their love could overcome any physical distance.

They were wrong.

They'd drifted apart, slowly, very slowly. But eventually they became strangers. Strangers who just happened to be married to one another. This peculiar, but seemingly stable, situation went on for four years. Then she fell in love with someone new. That's when everything fell apart. They were divorced within three months.

It had hurt. At times it had even hurt bad. But never as bad as Mark might have expected. Mostly it just seemed so unreal. He still had trouble believing it was true.

"I am sorry doctor," said Pasteur's comsys, "her Lieutenant says she is unavailable at the moment."

"Well, keep trying."

"As you wish. By the way, you asked that I let you know when we arrived at E-33. I am now placing us in a parking orbit around the planet. Bonaparte, having maneuvered Andromeda into an orbit a few hundred miles lower than ours, has just released it, and is moving to a higher orbit, perhaps geosynchronous. Military scout ships appear to be taking up strategic sentry positions in various low altitude—and therefore high speed—orbits."

Mark did not respond. He just stared at the caged hand.

During the course of the journey, he had shared with the military commander, everything he'd learned—usually the same day he'd learned it. And likewise, she'd shared with him everything she knew about the situation on E-33. The first frantic message torpedo from Livingstone had described an odd emergency; a second torpedo had added a number of truly bizarre details; but neither torpedo provided Mark with any answers, only more questions.

"People who sleep for weeks and can't be made to wake-up?" Mark said, suddenly. "Cuts that won't heal? Beards that wont grow? What kind of disease is this?"

The comsys said nothing. The question was obviously rhetorical.

Mark was under a great deal of stress and had become completely unable to sleep. He and his paramedics had spent the thirteen days of their journey studying tissue samples and running experiments. They'd soon learned that the hand wasn't the only thing aboard ship composed of artificial cells built and maintained by nano-robots: so were the undead.

Mark's first reaction was, *Why would nano-robots build dead bodies?* He had since developed some theories, but they were theories he found ugly and repulsive. He tried not to think about them. He failed. Often.

Mark stared at the hand. It was no longer just a hand now; and having outgrown the first cage, had been moved to a larger one. It had regenerated its arm all the way up to the shoulder joint.

"Why are the nano-robots doing this? When will they stop? Good Lord in Heaven, there must be limits! Will they try to grow a head on the thing? And if they do, will it be able to think? Will it... Will it remember?"

"Doctor," said Pasteur's comsys. "I'm having problems with electrical circuits numbers 17, 18 and 19."

PLAGUE AT REDHOOK

"What kind of problems?"

"17 has failed. 18 and 19 are experiencing voltage fluctuations: mostly surges and spikes. Wait. Now 19 has failed. Short circuits could explain—"

An alarm bell rang through the ship.

"I have detected a fire inside bulkhead forty-two!" said the comsys. "The automatic fire extinguishing system has been tripped!"

"How big a fire!?" Mark asked. "Is it spreading?"

The alarm stopped ringing.

"The fire is out."

Mark took a deep breath. "Good."

"Agreed. And this would explain the electrical problems. The fire must have burned through the insulation. Unfortunately, circuit 17 provides power for life-support."

"Oh?"

"Yes. That system is now inoperative. Ship's air will become stale within the hour and will be unbreatheable in approximately ten."

"What about the backup system?

"19 is the backup."

"You're kidding?"

"No," the comsys said flatly, as though unperturbed. "All humans must evacuate the ship."

"Evacuate? To where? We are under quarantine. Plague level! We'll just have to fix it."

"That is not an option. Repairs will require 45 hours."

"What? Where the Hell are we gonna go?"

"To the surface."

"Are you craz—" Mark froze in position; a confused look spread over his face. Somewhere, deep inside his mind, his *this-is-too-good-to-be-true* alarm started ringing. Could a comsys sabotage the ship it had been installed in? The very ship it was programmed to control and protect? He glanced down at the hand's shoulder joint. A smile spread slowly across his face. He shrugged and said, "Get me the commander."

Chapter 15

Welcome to E-33

Known for almost two centuries, the star which E-33 orbits had long been included in the Henry Draper Catalog as HD-45610 and the Smithsonian Astrophysical Observatory Star Catalog as SAO-196834. It is a solitary G0 main sequence star 74.98 light-years from Earth.

There are 50,965 stars closer to Earth, of which 3,567 are class G, but only 32 possess planets that have been officially designated as earth-like. 31 if you don't count Earth.

Forty-one years ago, in the summer of 2093, the husband and wife team of physicists, Jackson and Jackson developed the first human-made hyperlight drive. It was their little unmanned prototype which, traveling from Lunar orbit to Mars, first broke the light barrier.

Beginning five years later, six people from three continents spent two long years traveling the 4.4 light-years to Alpha Centauri. Their six year mission to examine the triple star system was an overwhelming success. And not just scientifically; it brought home the fact that other star systems

PLAGUE AT REDHOOK

were real places where real people could go and do real things. It sparked all of humanity with a desire to discover and explore strange new worlds.

The decades that followed were punctuated by sudden speed increases in the hyperlight drive. Each of which prompted an exploration boom-time. Cynics claimed this was just because no entrepreneur, corporation, or sovereign nation wanted to be left out of the race to claim new and valuable resources. But regardless of the reasons behind it, the fact remained that humanity was crawling all over itself trying to examine first-hand all the nearby star systems.

Even back then, when all the worlds we'd visited were too hot or too cold or too poisonous, astronomers predicted that eventually we would find a planet that was just right. A planet that was earth-like. The standard definition of earth-like has remained pretty much the same ever since: any world where you can safely walk around outside completely naked for hours at a time.

Stand-up comedians enjoyed pointing out that by this definition, Earth itself was not earth-like. That in most places nudity was prevented by climate or weather; and even when and where the weather permitted it, the police would not.

Even so, the popular definition stood, and twenty two years ago, the first genuinely earth-like planet was discovered and explored. Its colonization, however, was delayed eight years for fear of ecological impact to its indigenous life forms. This led directly to the forming of the United Nations Astrophysical Survey Organization (UN-ASO) to coordinate the systematic locating, surveying and colonizing of earth-like planets.

Seven years ago UN-ASO's newest and largest telescope—the 100 Meter Optical Telescope orbiting Saturn—spotted a planet 75 light-years from Earth that appeared to be *about* the right size, and orbiting *about* the right distance from its primary star to be earth-like. The planet was immediately given the designation PE-211, and placed at the very bottom of a very long list of maybes.

Four years later, a robotic probe the size of a small suitcase, arrived at PE-211 and entered a polar orbit. The probe examined the planet and its atmosphere in great detail; performing atmospheric chemical analysis, and creating geological maps in visible light, ultraviolet, and infrared; as well as by reflected radio waves of various frequencies.

The probe, however, did not land; and remained in orbit for just 23.1 hours (one planetary rotation) before heading off to the next of its twelve targets: PE-307.

At the conclusion of its mission, after the probe had visited all twelve possibly earth-like planets, and had returned to Earth to deliver the information it had collected, the results looked promising for only one of its targets. But, of course, even one is a large number when you're counting colonizeable worlds. The decision was made to send a human survey team.

Before the ill-fated survey team fell into their prolonged sleep, they succeeded in verifying that the planet was within official parameters to be legally designated earth-like, and so had raised its status and changed its name to E-33.

It was to this planet that Doctor Mark Tolman now descended.

* * *

Pasteur's little ambulance fell through a beautiful blue sky dotted with puffy white clouds. The craft resembled Gazelle's landers but was smaller, newer and more streamlined. It made a gentle landing on a thick carpet of red grass not more than a hundred feet from Zebra.

Mark stepped out through the door, squinting as his eyes adjusted to the bright sunlight. The sun on his arms and face felt warmer than he'd expected, but the breeze was soft and pleasant. Paramedic number one levitated out into the sunlight behind him.

Mark spotted two people approaching followed by a floating medsys. The lead person was a tall thin white-haired

PLAGUE AT REDHOOK

old man with long lanky arms and legs. A man Mark thought could probably have played Abe Lincoln in a modest community theater using no more makeup than black hair dye and a fake beard. Behind him was an attractive blonde-haired woman, with—she stopped and let out a violent sneeze—bright red eyes.

Old Mister Lincoln stopped in front of Mark and extended his right hand.

Mark shook it, and said, "The air tastes good here."

Abe smiled. "That was my first reaction too. I'm Tom Vickery: Captain of the Supply Ship Livingstone."

"Nice to meet you. I'm Mark Tolman, Doctor of Surgery, Chief of Medicine, and Captain of the U.N. Hospital Ship Louis Pasteur. And its only human crewmember, I might add." Mark looked around at the red, yellow and brown trees that surrounded this grassy plain. "You've found yourselves a beautiful planet on which to get quarantined."

Tom frowned up at the six tiny black dots spaced evenly around them, high in the blue sky. "You seem to have brought company."

Mark didn't look. He knew they were assault robots; hovering, monitoring, ready to enforce the quarantine—by force, obviously—on a split second's notice. "Yes. I'm afraid so. But we mustn't let them spoil the moment."

"Agreed." Tom smiled and waved to the woman, who appeared to be holding back another sneeze. "Let me introduce you to Blair Englewood, and of course, our medsys." Blair nodded at the mention of her name, while the medsys simply floated a smidgen lower, as though affecting a mechanical curtsy. "My engineers are under sedation at the moment," Tom added. "Their symptoms are a bit more extreme."

"I'm eager to talk with each of your party, but I should probably start with your medsys for an overall assessment—" He froze in position.

"Doctor?" said Tom. "Is something wrong?"

"Huh? No. One of my paramedics is paging me from the ship. I hate to appear rude, but would you excuse me, please? It sounds as though it may be important."

"Certainly." Tom raised a hand, in the stop gesture. "It's quite all right."

Mark stepped back inside the ambulance and closed the door.

"You were correct, Doctor," said the voice of number two. "I would never have believed it, but it's true. Every cell in her body. Every last cell!"

Mark's face grew tense. "Damn!" He made a fist, then realized he had no idea who or what to shake it at. "That's not what I wanted to hear," he said, and paused to regain his composure. The first step of which involved coaxing his fist open and dropping it at his side. "How is she?"

"As sex-crazed as ever."

"She has no idea?"

"I don't know. She speaks of nothing but sex."

"Of course; of course." Mark nodded. "I want her brought down here. I'll send the ambulance back up for her."

"Yes, Doctor," the machine said, just before Mark signed off.

During the next few hours Mark interviewed Livingstone's crew and medsys. He learned everything he could about the plague, but revealed nothing he had discovered. He didn't want to create a panic.

Some symptoms were as unmistakable as those of the passionate-woman. The sleepers were still sleeping, and Blair's twenty-four hour flu was now two weeks old. Barb and Sammy—when brought out of their sedation—were still laughing and crying respectively.

But everyone's biggest concern seemed focused on Barb's baby. It was a full month overdue, and the medsys insisted it hadn't grown an ounce in the last fourteen days.

PLAGUE AT REDHOOK

Mark took blood, saliva, and tissue samples from Tom's crew; and carefully examined each sample under the electron microscope. There was no mistake.

Chapter 16

Bad Tidings

"That's ridiculous," said Tom as he shifted his weight in the deeply-padded easy chair inside Zebra's dining room. He turned from Mark and looked at Blair sitting in an identical chair next to him. She looked shocked; perhaps too shocked to speak. He turned back to Mark. "It's crazy. It doesn't make any sense."

Mark, standing near the door, spoke softly. "I wish you were right."

Tom waved both hands in a display of disbelief. "How can microscopic robots replace all the cells in our bodies without our even feeling it? It's nuts. Totally nuts."

"I'm not claiming to understand it. I'm only saying it's happened. The evidence it undeniable."

Blair blurted out, "Well, I don't feel artificial!"

"It will take time to accept, I'm sure."

The medsys, now resting on a low table, asked gravely, "Doctor, as a result of this condition, has anyone died?"

The room fell silent.

PLAGUE AT REDHOOK

Tom and Blair glanced at the machine, then stared at Mark.

He almost told them about the hand, but held his tongue. Instead, he said very carefully, "Not to the best of my knowledge."

There was more silence.

Then the medsys asked, "Have you tested yourself for this condition?"

"No," Mark said, quickly.

"Do you intend to?"

"Not until I work up the courage."

"May I ask why?"

He looked around the room. Every eye was on him, and every eye seemed to have lost hope. He made an effort to stand a little straighter, a little taller. His patients needed a show of bravery. He felt as though he might need one too. "Because I already know what the result will be."

Chapter 17

Who

Day 22

High above the quarantined planet, in an orbit that matched this world's daily rotation rate, sailed the warship Bonaparte. Black and windowless and shaped like a manta ray, it carried missiles and particle beam weapons sufficient to completely decimate an unprotected world.

A quartet of smaller scout ships, with fully robotic crews—and consequently no life-support systems at all—but which otherwise matched Bonaparte for shape, color and destructive potential, and which were normally tucked under its motherly manta wings, were now deployed in four crisscrossing orbits at lower altitudes. They watched with unblinking robotic eyes for any attempt, by anyone or anything, to enter or leave the atmosphere of the planet below.

These five ships were currently on yellow alert—pretending to not exist. This involved more than a simplistic radio silence: their hyperlight drives were shut down altogether, electric gyros were used for attitude control instead of jets of heated gas, and their entire hulls were cryogenically chilled to

PLAGUE AT REDHOOK

2.7 degrees above absolute zero to make their infrared emission spectra match that of the blackness of space.

Inside Bonaparte, the bridge was dimly lit, almost to the point of foreboding. The scattered dots, lines and arcs of multi-colored light emanating from the various control panels added to the look of power and strict formality. The room's color scheme was glossy black with shining gold trim and was designed specifically to appear reminiscent of a military dress uniform. It worked. Even the black and gold cleaning robots preformed their menial chores while marching at attention. They moved in crisp formation, like tiny drill teams practicing ancient maneuvers.

Commander Dorothy Ponder studied, intently, the little computer display panel mounted on the arm of her large black command chair. Almost imperceptibly, she stroked her fingers across the smooth cloth of the padded arm rests. Her nails, cleanly manicured earlier that day by a small grooming robot, were as short and unpolished as those of most men. She wore no decorative jewelry except for a single class ring; and only that because she'd attended Annapolis.

The little computer display listed the people currently on the planet's surface, and the status of their symptoms. She reviewed Doctor Tolman's report describing the nano-robots and the artificial cells which they seemed to make.

She looked up at the bridge's main display. At the moment it showed a map of the star system she was in. It detailed the orbits and locations of seven planets, thirty four moons, and several thousand asteroids. Each of these naturally occurring objects was labeled with a newly assigned numerical designation. Not one of them was dignified with a name.

Lieutenant alpha, her robotic helmsman, turned its vaguely human form away from its control panel to face her. "Commander," it said, creating vibrations in the air using a small speaker mounted behind a grillwork where its mouth should have been. When the robot observed that it had obtained the commander's attention, it continued: "The human doctor, Mark Tolman, wishes to speak with you."

The commander opened her mouth, and spoke using similar vibrations. "Put him through."

"Aye aye," said the machine, and turned back to its control panel.

The military, with its centuries of tradition, had been slow to accept the newfangled concept of computer implants. Though many officers and enlisted personnel possessed them, all orders were still given by open verbalization. By living in such a quaintly backward organization, Dorothy Ponder, despite her rank, status and financial stability, still had no computer implanted inside her skull. Consequently she was forced to rely on whatever crude vocalizations she could produce with her mouth, and upon her ship's primitive high-resolution full-color three-dimensional display screens.

Doctor Tolman's face appeared on the little display by her right arm. She realized immediately that he was looking into a mirror, and that this image was actually coming to her, by way of his implanted PC—from his own eyes.

"Yes, doctor?" she said.

"Commander, I have been examining the nano-robots and have come to the conclusion that they are more advanced than any available commercially, or for medical use. Which leaves only the possibility that they are a new military design. Do you have any knowledge of such a military project?"

"No, Doctor. I thought of that myself—the day you first described them to me—and I have already investigated that possibility. My superiors assure me these nano-robots were not made by any U.N. funded military project."

Mark hesitated only briefly. "Do you believe them?"

There was a moment of silence.

"I believe that they believe it."

"I see."

There was another moment of silence.

PLAGUE AT REDHOOK

"Doctor, I've read your reports; these nano-robots seem very advanced. I'm not convinced that any group of human scientists, regardless of their funding, could have produced them."

Mark frowned slightly. "What are you saying?"

"I'm saying that, as you study them, you should consider that they may be of alien origin."

Lieutenants alpha and sigma both turned from their control panels to look at their commander.

It was common knowledge, that with the exception of one brief encounter, nearly a hundred years ago, when extremely cold-bodied methane-based aliens had surrounded Earth for several terrifying days, no human had ever seen an intelligent alien. And that since that one encounter, no additional aliens have shown themselves; be they hot, cold or lukewarm.

Mark tried to speak, but stumbled for words. "I. . ."

The commander interrupted, "I'm not saying that they must be of alien manufacture. Only that it is something we should keep in mind."

"Um. Thank you Commander. I. . . I'll think about that."

The doctor's face disappeared from the little screen.

Lieutenant sigma, the robotic weapons officer, said, "Commander, do you truly believe they are alien?"

She did not look at the robot. Instead she closed her eyes, leaned back in her black command chair, and expelled a huge breath of air. "I sure as Hell hope not. This mess is ugly enough without dragging aliens into it."

Chapter 18

Seduction

Tom stood behind Mark, curious about the young Doctor's work, and wishing there was some way he could help—other than just staying out of the way.

Mark was seated on a tall stool hunched over tissue samples and his electron microscope. Assisted by paramedic number one, he was running more tests on the samples they had taken from Tom and his crew.

Tom glanced around the room. Most of the lab benches in Zebra's bio-lab were covered with blankets upon which lay inanimate bodies. Mark referred to these people as the undead. Tom did not see the hand, nor did he know of its existence. Mark had it hidden in a corner, inside a large cage covered with a white bed sheet.

During his first twenty-four hours on the planet's surface, Mark had set up shop in Zebra's bio-lab. Now he both worked and lived in this one big room. He had explained to Tom that the ambulance would have been far too small. He needed enough room to keep a close eye on his most bizarre patients. If

PLAGUE AT REDHOOK

there had been more room in the bio-lab he probably would have kept the passionate-woman in there as well; instead she was kept under sedation and placed with the sleepers aboard Elk.

Mark had moved the ambulance to just outside Zebra's rear loading doors; this was because some of its specialized medical equipment had proven to be less than portable. And true to Murphy's law, the very items he needed most seemed to be those with the least portability.

As Tom watched Mark work, he repeatedly felt the call of nature. For the last three weeks this call had become a proverbial thorn in his side; or as he'd described it to Mark: a pain in his butt. He could never be certain if he really needed to pee, or if it was just the phantom sensation that wouldn't go away. He'd quickly developed a habit of going to the privy with unusual frequency.

He tapped Mark on the shoulder. "Excuse me. I'll be back in a few minutes."

Mark looked up from his tissue samples just long enough to smile slightly and nod.

Tom stepped out through Zebra's wide-open rear loading doors and into the warm sunlight of another monotonously beautiful day, then walked around the ambulance parked outside.

Having been born and raised on the overpopulated planet Earth, Tom had always taken a peculiar delight in answering the call of nature while surrounded by nature itself, out in the great outdoors. So naturally, on this nearly deserted world, he took a short walk into the red-leafed forest and located a thirsty-looking tree upon which to bestow his nutritious gift of life.

As he finished spraying the trunk, he felt someone, very lightly, touch his back. He glanced around—as best he could without turning enough to display his privates—but didn't see anyone. As he hurried to get all of himself back into his pants, a female voice whispered into his mind, "Don't turn around. Not yet."

He didn't recognize the voice. It wasn't Barb. Could it be Blair? "Who are you?" he asked.

She cooed, softly, "What are names?"

Tom felt her hands slide up and down his spine; slowly, as though massaging. He was about to pull away, when he noticed a surprising feeling of warmth spreading through his chest. Her touch had caused it. And he liked it. He liked it a lot.

Her hands reached around him and began caressing his chest. The warmth grew stronger. She hugged him, pressing the front of her body against his back. He could feel the shape of her, of her hips and breasts. He reached up and stroked her forearms on his chest. She squeezed him tightly.

He took one of her hands, raised it to his mouth and kissed it. It smelled sweet and completely unfamiliar. The nails were long and painted red. Not Blair; her nails are short and painted pink. He didn't care who it was. His lust was strong.

He turned around. He didn't recognize her, but he didn't care. She was beautiful, and she was already naked.

She reached her face up toward his; he reached his down toward hers; they kissed. They caressed and kissed, and kissed and caressed, and just as she began to remove his shirt, he had a flash-back to a terrible icy field under a heavy black sky.

His hands stopped caressing, and his lips stopped kissing. Hers didn't, and hers didn't. But his did.

She writhed her body against his. She moaned, "Don't stop. I'm ready for you. I am soooo ready!"

But all Tom could think of was how cold and alone his true love was. Of how far apart they were; separated by time and space. His heart ached.

He turned from the strange woman and ran. When she called after him, he ran all the faster. He ran though the trees of the alien forest like a wild animal. Red leaves and yellow branches slashed at his face and hair. He ran until his steps were clumsy and his stride was ragged; he fell forward and caught himself leaning against a tree.

He looked up to the blue sky with tears in his eyes and spoke a single word. The one word that summed up all his longings and all his dreams and all his hopes for all his life. He spoke it by forcing a great breath of air out through his teeth and lips. "Maggie!"

Chapter 19

Controlled Experiments

Perched on his lab stool, Mark raised a small hand mirror to his face and said, "Commander, I and paramedic number one have spent the last few hours searching for the source of this nano-robotic plague. We have examined, under the electron microscope, tissue samples taken from the bright red alien grass that seems to grow everywhere down here, as well as from every species of alien tree we've been able to locate. The results are the same for all species. Every living thing within this planet's biosphere is composed entirely of artificial cells maintained by countless nano-robots."

"What's more," he continued, "these nano-robots seem to exist everywhere. They permeate the soil like microbes; drift about in pond water like amoebae; and are wafted about in the air like a fine dust. And just as dust will adhere to every exposed surface, so too the nano-robots have accumulated on the exterior surface of everything."

"Somehow, I am not surprised by this," she said.

"In retrospect, it does seem logical," Mark said, with a slow sad nod. "Everyone who landed on this planet contaminated

PLAGUE AT REDHOOK

themselves with amazing rapidity. Walking on the grass spread nano-robots on their shoes and lower clothing. Everything they touched got them on their hands. Even while standing motionless they settled on their skin as dust. But the worst contamination occurred as they breathed. Every time they inhaled, they sucked more and more nano-robots straight into the very core of their body. The microscopic robots soon coated the walls of their mouth, throat, trachea and lungs. And once inside the lungs, nothing separated them from the bloodstream except a thin membrane just a few cells thick. And of course, once they'd entered the blood, the swiftly flowing fluid carried them into every vital organ: heart, muscles, bones, nervous system, and. . . and the brain." Mark blinked a few times and moistened his lips nervously. He found himself imagining how easily the nano-robots had invaded his own body.

The commander said nothing; apparently waiting for him to recover.

Mark hid his mouth with the fingers of one hand for a moment, then removed them. "For the sake of thoroughness," he said, suddenly, "we examined samples of rock and soil. We found nano-robots scattered throughout the soil, and covering the surfaces of the rocks. However, they had not penetrated into any rock's solid interior. So we examined the metallic and plastic surfaces of paramedic number one, and of the lander Elk. They too were covered with nano-robots, but none had burrowed into their surfaces or had penetrated them in any way. We concluded from this that the nano-robots will attack—or replace, if you prefer—only organic tissues. That is to say, tissues composed of living cells. And that they will ignore anything they perceive to be inorganic or *non*-living, such as a robot, a spacecraft, or a rock. To test this theory, and other ideas I have about them, I'd like you to have an uncontaminated assault robot bring a few things down to me from your ship."

After Mark explained what items he wanted and why he wanted them, the commander agreed. And soon Mark was running his experiments.

He started by placing an uninfected house plant from Commander Ponder's private quarters—a small cactus—next to a clump of the local red grass, which he'd gathered from outside Zebra's rear door.

Within ten minutes the surface of the uninfected house plant was crawling with hundreds of thousands of nano-robots. Though even in such numbers they remained invisible to the naked eye. The only noticeable change was that the cactus's surface seemed ever so slightly darkened, as if it were in shadow.

Within ten minutes more, Mark observed that the nano-robots had begun disassembling the natural organic cells that composed the plant's outer skin, and had begun constructing artificial cells in their place. Within ten minutes more they were inside the cactus's circulatory system, working their way into every part of the plant.

Mark tried different plant species from Bonaparte, lilies, carnations, Venus's-flytrap, but always got the same result. It seemed the nano-robots made no judgment over which life-forms they would make artificial. He even tried tricking them with plastic roses. They were not fooled. The roses remained plastic.

The experiments showed the nano-robots to be more than just persistent in their work; they were openly aggressive. Few barriers succeed in preventing them from fulfilling their goal. Yet, for some reason, they were just as aggressive at not disturbing anything not composed of living cells. Even when the only way to get to a living thing was to cut their way through an inorganic barrier, they would not make a hole. Mark was certain they had the ability to cut holes, so he decided this must be some kind of taboo—something they were prohibited from doing by their original programming. At least this would explain why Tom's medsys, as well as other robots and computers, had experienced no damage.

Mark isolated individual nano-robots and tested their basic intelligence. Individually, they proved to be exceedingly stupid, but they showed an ability to coordinate their actions somewhat, when a number of them were treated as a group.

Chapter 20

Biological Warfare

The commander smiled pleasantly at the face on the main display screen on her bridge. "Thank you, Doctor," she said when Mark seemed to have finished explaining everything he had learned. "Please keep me informed of any further information you are able to uncover. This is Commander Ponder, out and clear."

The moment the human doctor's face disappeared, the smile on the commander's face disappeared too.

"Lieutenant alpha!" She barked, loud and crisp.

"Sir!" it shouted back.

"Raise the status of this ship and all orbiting ships to red alert."

"Aye aye!"

"Lieutenant Sigma!"

"Sir!"

"I want you to scan every inch of that planet below for indications of intelligent alien activity! Radio frequency emissions; excess infrared heat radiation; buildings or structures that cannot be explained by natural means, such as: volcanism, plate-tectonics, mountain building, erosion, etc. Do not—I repeat—Do not assume the structures will be easily found. They may in fact be well hidden, perhaps even underground. And I want reports of this search-in-progress every five minutes. Do you understand?"

"Aye aye!"

The commander leaned back in her command chair with an expression of deep annoyance on her face. "Nothing the doctor has found changes the likelihood that the nano-robots are of alien origin. And this whole thing is beginning to stink. Stink to the highest Heaven. It's time to plan for the worst."

"Stink? sir."

"Yeah. Stink! Like some kind of nano-tech version of germ-warfare."

Chapter 21

The Twitch

Day 23

Mark placed a fresh tissue sample into a little metal frame, then slid the frame into the electron microscope's tiny airlock. As he listened to the chugging of the machine pumping air from its airlock, he realized Blair was standing next to him.

"Doctor," she said, softly, "I want to ask you something. If I may."

He was puzzled by her clumsy choice of phrasing: asking permission to ask a question. And by the paradoxical concept itself: asking to ask. He decided this indicated some kind of overwhelming reluctance. Was she afraid of offending him? Afraid she might not like his answer? Or, worst of all, afraid of what she might learn?

"What is it?" he prompted.

"I. . ." She faltered. "I was in here yesterday, while you were out, and. . ." She looked away, avoiding his eyes. "I know I shouldn't have. But I snooped around and. . ." She glanced into the bio-lab's far corner. The corner where Mark had hidden the hand. She whispered, "I found something. It scared me. I tried to forget. But I can't stop thinking about it." She looked Mark straight in the eye. "I want you to tell me what it is."

Mark spoke softly, "Can you describe it?"

Slowly and deliberately, she said, "It was an arm. It was only an arm, but it was alive. I saw it move."

Mark glanced at the corner, then back to her. "Have you mentioned this to Tom? Or to the medsys?"

She shook her head only once. "No."

"Good. I intend to tell the medsys as soon as I know more about it, but I'm concerned how news of it might effect Tom. He has too much to worry about as it is. His stress level is already too high."

Mark told Blair most of what he knew about the hand; that it had been just a hand when he'd found it, that it was rebuilding itself, and that he didn't know when it would stop. She was properly shocked by all this, but promised not to tell.

Before she left, she walked back into its corner and lifted one edge of the sheet which Mark used to hide it from the bio-lab's more casual visitors. She took a long careful look, then dropped the sheet, gave Mark a shaky smile, and left the lab without a word.

Returning to his work, Mark glanced at the bio-lab's far wall and spent a split second imagining that a large clock hung there. The wall bore no such clock, nor were there any clocks of any kind anywhere inside Zebra. Even so, a phantom clock appeared on the wall, lingering just long enough for Mark to learn what time it was, before disappearing.

"PC," he said, "ask number one to hurry back with those samples. I don't know what's taking it so long. It's been gone more than an hour."

"As you wish," his PC said. "By the way, Tom is calling you."

"I'm awfully busy here. Tell him. . . No, wait. It might be important. Put him through."

Tom's voice entered his mind. "Mark, I've found something I think you should look at. It's in the forest about three hundred feet behind Zebra."

"I'm pretty busy, Tom. Can you look at it to me?"

Tom hesitated a moment, then said, "OK"

When the image from Tom's eyes entered Mark's mind, he almost fell off his lab stool. In the scarlet grass, inches from Tom's feet, lay number one—broken, smashed, inert. The toe of one of Tom's black shoes poked at the robotic corpse. It did not react.

"PC!" Mark said. "Contact number one."

A few seconds passed in silence.

"I'm sorry, but number one does not respond on any com channel. It would seem the paramedic is dead."

"Who would do—" but Mark interrupted his own question with the answer. "Of course. The mad-woman. But I thought her PC would blind her if she tried to break the law. Destroying a paramedic is certainly unlawful."

"That's what her PC told my medsys," Tom said. "She must have discovered a way to keep it from blinding her."

"I don't see how. It's implanted inside her skull. The batteries can't run down—they're charged electrochemically using the chemicals coursing through her own bloodstream. Being artificial wont prevent the charging; the nano-robots mimic our normal blood-chemistry too closely for that."

"I don't know how she could have done it either," Tom said. "All I know is, she's the only person on this planet crazy enough to kill. And this," Tom poked at number one again, "this is a dead robot. You add it up; see if you get anything different."

The image Mark saw coming in from Tom, began shaking violently. Then a hand came up and blocked the view from one eye. Tom shouted, "Cut it out!"

Mark squinted—as if this might help him see more clearly through Tom's eyes. "What's going on? Cut what out?"

"Not you. My eye. It's twitching again. Been doing it off and on all day. It's driving me nuts!"

"Let me see."

Tom pulled a small round mirror out of his shirt pocket and raised it to his eyes.

Mark examined the old face. "Move it closer, please. Yes, that's better."

Only one of Tom's green eyes was visible in the tiny mirror. Suddenly, the loose wrinkled skin under that eye jerked toward the man's nose, moving nearly a quarter of an inch. It jerked several times in rapid succession, then paused a few seconds before doing it again.

"Does it hurt?"

"No. But it tickles like crazy."

"Have you had your medsys look at it?"

"Not yet."

"PC, call Tom's medsys. Tell it to go to him at once."

"As you wish." A second later. "It is on its way. ETA: three minutes."

"Good." Mark glanced at his microscope and samples. "I want it to examine you. This may be a new symptom." When Mark looked back, Tom was again looking down. Mark's former helper was in view. "And I'd better let the commander know what's happened to number one." Mark sighed. "This mad-woman may turn out to be more trouble than I'd expected."

Chapter 22

Craters

Lieutenant sigma turned and faced its commander. "Sir, I have found no evidence that intelligent aliens are currently active on or near the planet. No artificial structures, and no energy emissions. However, I have found evidence of alien activity in the past."

"Explain," the commander said.

"Global mapping surveys show the planet-wide network of rolling hills are actually highly eroded craters. Their residual radiation levels indicate these craters were all made by nuclear detonations, and their non-random distribution pattern indicate they were aimed at specific targets."

The commander pounded her armrests with both fists. "War!"

"Exactly," said the machine, calmly. "In my estimation, roughly one hundred thousand years ago the planet's biosphere was nuked into near oblivion."

"Damn! I knew it! I could almost smell it." She sucked air through clenched teeth. "So there was a war here. The nano-robots must be a remnant of that war."

"That is very possible."

Chapter 23

Naked PC

Outside, on the red lawn in front of Zebra, Tom sat on a tall lab stool. The medsys—open, with its interior exposed—hovered in front of him. Its many lights focused their warmth on the skin below his eye. Mark stood beside it, staring at the brightly illuminated spot on Tom's face.

They were all three waiting for the twitch.

Tom noticed an assault robot—about the size of a medsys, but black and bristling with weapons pointing in every direction. It floated motionless, fifteen feet up in the air, some twenty feet behind Mark's back. Since the death of number one, they'd moved to lower altitudes; guarding the landers and occasionally following people around. Probably to protect them. Probably.

Tom stared at the deadly black object. He tried to make out detail on its surface, but soon decided he was wasting his time. It was too black. In fact, to only say it was black, fell far short of the true depth of its blackness. In broad daylight not a glint

PLAGUE AT REDHOOK

or a sheen escaped its surface. In the full light of the sun it was a featureless silhouette; a hole in the sky; a hole full of nothing.

The assault robot suddenly spun about and dived at the ground behind Mark. It came to a sharp stop four feet above the red grass and shouted as though angry enough to kill. "Halt! Who goes there!"

The medsys, which had been blocking Tom's view, turned in time for Tom to see Blair—who had apparently been running toward the little group—stop too fast and fall backward, landing flat on her butt. Her hair and breasts bounced as she hit the grass, but it looked too painful for Tom to think it sexy.

"It's me, you idiot!" she yelled.

The black machine swooped in closer, floating low over her chest; as if pinning a wrestling opponent to the mat. It was inches from her chin, almost between her breasts.

"Who is 'Me'!?"

"Blair, you moron! Are you blind? Get off me or, I swear, I'll sneeze snot all over you! And don't think I can't. My nose has got a hair trigger and I'm loaded for bear!"

The machine's voice changed to a drab mono-tone indicating it had lost interest in her. "Voice-print analysis matches facial characteristics and retina print. Blair Englewood, you are free to get up." And with that it floated higher, returning to its lookout position.

Blair lifted herself from the ground and shook loose whatever dirt might have clung to her clothing. "Damn, you'd think I was bringing you a bomb."

"Are you all right?" Mark asked.

"I think so. Doctor, is this what I think it is?" She held up a small object with a complicated tangle of fine wires dangling from around its edges. The wires—and there were hundreds—varied in length, but not in thickness; they were all thinner than human hair. The object itself was a single piece of white plastic, shaped like a flat disk, but curved as though cut from the surface of a soccer ball.

Mark frowned and reached for it. She placed it in his hand. The medsys floated close over Mark's shoulder, positioning itself to see the object better. Mark examined it carefully. "Yes. Yes, it is." He rubbed his chin. "Where did you find it?"

"It was laying on the ground, under the trees, on the far side of Elk. I nearly stepped on it."

"PC, can you contact this unit?"

"I'm sorry, Doctor, it does not respond."

Blair leaned forward. "But it is a PC?"

"Oh, yes. Without a doubt." Mark nodded. "It's just not functioning. Ether it's broken, or its batteries are dead. My first theory would be that the mad-woman must have—"

"This unit's serial number," interrupted the medsys, "matches that of Doctor Sharon Rice's personal computer." The serial number it was referring to was embossed on the object's curved surface.

Mark nodded again. "Just as I thought," he said softly. "She must have removed it from her head."

Tom blinked wild-eyed. "Removed it?" he squawked. "Removed it? Are you crazy? Those things are implanted surgically! And not just under the skin, but inside a hollow in the skull. Inside a marrow chamber. You can't just cut through the scalp and yank it out. You've got to break bones to get to it!" He waived his hands frantically for emphasis. "And even if she could get her hands on it, the wires run to all different parts of the brain. Yanking it out would slice the brain in a hundred places! Mark, you of all people should know that removing it without tools and surgical equipment. . ." Tom shook his head spasmodically; desperate to fill the gap as he searched for words of more persuasive power. "Well. . . It's impossible! It's just plain impossible!"

Mark gave Tom his most compassionate look. The same look a veterinarian might give a dog just before putting it to sleep forever. He placed his hand on Tom's shoulder. "The fact that it's impossible is the very reason I believe that it's true"

Tom stared at him. Mouth open. Dumbfounded.

"If it really is hers," said the medsys, "then it can no longer protect us from her attacks."

Again Mark nodded. "As evidenced by her destruction of number one."

Tom's eye started twitching. He fought an impulse to rub it vigorously with both hands. Instead, he squinted and involuntarily raised one shoulder. "Medsys, the twitch is back."

The medsys turned toward Tom and directed its examination lights to the skin below his eye. Tom watched through the medsys's robotic eyes while—as it had done previously—the tiny patch of skin jerked sideways several times in rapid succession. Then it stopped.

"That's an odd coincidence," muttered the medsys, as though trying to imitate a human doctor confused about some minor thing.

"What's odd?" asked Tom.

"Well, it's not such a big—" The twitch started again, and the medsys fell silent.

Tom, and Mark, and even Blair, leaned forward to watch as Tom's face twitched and paused and twitched and paused; again and again; each burst of twitching lasting longer than the one before. Finally, after several minutes, the twitching stopped for a long stretch.

"There's something peculiar about that twitch," said the medsys. "Something familiar, and yet elusive. I can't quite put my finger. . ." The medsys's voice trailed off to nothing for a few seconds. Then it blurted out, "No! It can't be!"

"What!? What's wrong!?" Tom asked. He looked at Mark for help, but Mark could only shrug; eyebrows raised as high as they would go.

"Impossible!" shouted the medsys. "It's simply impossible!"

"What's impossible?" Tom demanded.

The medsys lowered its voice to a normal tone—perhaps having realized that it was frightening its patient. "Captain," it

Stephen Euin Cobb

said, softly. "Do you know the first seventy-two prime numbers?"

"No."

"Well, your twitch does. It has just counted them out in base six."

Chapter 24

Cratered Mantle

"Commander," said Lieutenant sigma, "I find myself deeply puzzled. I am accumulating facts that do not fit the theory that this planet has suffered a war. Or at least not a war as we understand them."

"Explain."

"This planet's outer crust is approximately twenty five miles thick—a typical figure for earth-like planets. Below that, the mantle is also of typical thickness—about two hundred miles. What is not typical, is that the upper surface of this planet's mantle is cratered."

"Cratered?"

"Yes. There are just over seventeen thousand impact craters on the mantle; all buried under twenty five miles of crustal rock. What's more, these craters are not randomly placed, instead they are arranged in a uniform grid pattern that stretches from pole to pole. No spot is left untouched."

"That is strange, I'll grant; but it still fits the theory."

"Sir, I must respectfully disagree. As we understand war, the goal is to disable the enemy to the point where they either surrender, or if unwilling to surrender, are no longer capable of continued aggression."

"So?" The commander shrugged. "This one was overkill. So what?"

"Sir. If you please. These seventeen thousand detonations blew the entire planet's crust—millions of cubic miles of rock—hundreds of miles up into the sky. The chunks of rock then followed suborbital paths, falling back to the surface over the course of about an hour. During the time that the rock was falling—up and then down—it was subjected to thousands of further detonations which raised its temperature above the melting point of aluminum. It is my opinion that this was not simply an attempt to destroy the inhabitants of a biosphere, but to destroy the biosphere itself. Whoever did this was trying to—"

The commander sprang out of her chair. "To kill the nano-robots! To kill them all in one big move!"

"Yes, sir. Exactly. I would conjecture that the aliens who did this did not originate on this planet, but were more likely exploring or colonizing it when they discovered its nano-robotic infestation. I might even hypothesize that once they themselves had become infected, they tried to protect the rest of their kind by suicidally blowing up the biosphere. Unfortunately, whatever the details of their situation, their attempt at purging the planet of nano-robots failed."

The commander eased back down into her chair, and began ignoring the robot's further analysis. *Can we succeed where they failed?* she thought, privately. *Do we have the weaponry?* She squinted. *This could be the first good field test of the new carbon-fusion warhead.*

The robot was saying, "The fact that at least some nano-robots survived the massive electromagnetic pulses created by thousands of nuclear detonations, indicates that a nano-robots' computer brain and internal nervous system does not use a circuitry based on electronics. Instead, they may use something similar to our optical computers, or perhaps a technology even more advanced." It then went on to say something about how the attempted destruction of the biosphere explained why the planet currently displayed so little variety in its lifeforms. Presumably, millions of plant and animal species were all made extinct in only one day.

The commander stood. "Thank you, Lieutenant. You've done an excellent job." She turned, walked off the bridge and retired to her quarters. There, she prepared an encoded message to torpedo to her superiors at Fort Delk—the SpaceGuard Regional Command Base on Big Sandy. In it, she described the situation, and requested operational guidelines. In her heart she knew what she was really asking: "Under what circumstances shall I destroy this planet's biosphere?"

Chapter 25

Black Wall of Death

Mark, the medsys and Blair were still gathered around Tom, who was still sitting on a tall lab stool on the red grass in front of Zebra. The open medsys, with its lights focused just below Tom's eye, hovered so close to its subject that Mark and Blair had to crane their necks to watch for the twitch.

The medsys reached out a frail, but beautifully glistening, gold-plated arm and proceeded to tap on the skin under Tom's eye.

Tom squirmed.

"Please, hold still," the machine said.

"Well, quit tickling me!"

"That will not be easy. You're such a wiggly-worm."

Mark raised a hand to cover a sudden smile.

Tom bristled at the machine. "Are you making fun of me?"

"Not at all," the medsys said. "Just trying to be more colorful; trying to use a metaphor now and again. I understand many patients prefer it. Make's the doctor seem more human."

"Well, cut it out. I don't like it. Besides you're too human as it is."

"As you wish."

The medsys tapped out a pattern of prime numbers on the skin under Tom's other eye. The one that had not been twitching.

A few seconds later, the twitching eye repeated this new pattern exactly as the medsys had tapped it out.

"That's good," Mark said. "But not conclusive. Try a pattern the twitch has never done before. Try tapping the mantissa of Pi."

"Good idea," the medsys said. "An endless string of digits known to all technologically advanced—"

"Just do it," Tom snapped, "You're beginning to bug me."

"OK; OK; no need to get your panties in a. . ."

"My what?"

"Never mind."

"My what?"

"Never mind!" The medsys tapped for almost a minute, then stopped and waited. "I did the first fifteen digits. That should be more than enough for them to figure out—"

Tom's eye started twitching.

The medsys fell silent.

"Well?" asked Tom.

The medsys remained silent, still counting the twitches.

"Well?" Tom asked again.

Still the medsys said nothing.

The twitches continued, on and on and on.

Tom said "Well?!"

The twitches stopped.

After ten or fifteen seconds had passed with no resumption of twitching, the medsys backed away from Tom, rather like a human straightening up after a difficult task. It said, softly, "They got it."

Mark brought his hands together with a loud clap and jumped with delight. "I knew it! I knew they could do it." But then he stopped suddenly and his face took on a troubled expression. "Wait. Did they simply repeat the pattern you tapped out?"

"No. After I did the first fifteen digits, they did the *next* fifteen."

Mark nodded his head vigorously and smiled wide enough to show every tooth. "They're organizing; trying to make sense of us. Trying to make sense of the new environment our bodies represent to them."

"What are you talking about?" asked Tom.

"Don't you see?" Mark waved his hands toward the grass and the trees. "The nano-robots have been building nothing but plants; they don't know how to operate animal bodies. Bodies with changing thoughts and behaviors and emotions. It's all new to them. My theory is that their creators designed and programmed them to help living things live longer healthier lives. If I'm right, our strange symptoms exist only because, when it comes to us, they don't know how to do their job properly. If we can communicate with them; explain what they are doing wrong—or more importantly, how to do it right—then the symptoms should disappear. My biggest worry is that they may not be smart enough for us to communicate with. And while this doesn't prove they are, at least it's a good sign. At least we know they're trying to. . . to. . ." Mark stared at Tom's arm.

"What's wrong?" Tom asked.

"I never noticed that before."

"What?"

"Your tattoo."

"I don't have a tattoo."

Mark pointed. "Then what's that on your arm?"

Tom lifted his right hand and found a complicated network of dark lines on the back side of his forearm. His mouth dropped open and he started making a low gurgling noise as if he might be choking on his own saliva.

The medsys drew near. "Do not fear, Captain. I'm sure this is simply the nano-robots trying a new method of communication."

"What do you think it means?" Mark asked. "Is it some kind of writing?"

"They would surely not expect us to decode their writing with so small a sample," said the medsys. "It is more likely a picture or pictograph—though of what I have no idea."

Blair pointed past Tom's shoulder, and yelled, "It's the man!"

Mark yelled, "Don't let him get away!" and started running.

Tom turned around in his seat to look, but only saw Mark's back as he ran in the general direction of Zebra's rear. Tom jumped to his feet to follow Mark, but bumped into Blair who apparently had the same idea.

Mark rounded Zebra's rear, stopped suddenly, and yelled, "The other way!" He pointed. "There he goes!"

The medsys flew upward, rolling itself into its closed ball-shape as it rose. It then curved its path into a horizontal line and stopped to hover twenty feet above Zebra.

Mark trotted around the back of Zebra, and into Tom's view. He was panting and his black hair was a mess. "Where did he go?"

"Don't kill him!" shouted the medsys frantically, just before it swooped down in a ground-skimming arc from its elevated vantage point. "It's not his fault!" The machine curved to the right and disappeared behind the lander Elk.

Mark ran toward Elk. Blair and Tom followed.

When Tom rounded Elk's tail, he saw four jet-black assault robots surrounding a terrified man in filthy ragged clothing. They didn't just hover around him, they circled him at high speed, forming an impenetrable fence about him—a wall of death.

The man turned this way and that, searching frantically for an escape. The look on his face suggested that he was on the verge of panic; and that his panic was likely to manifest itself in a burst of wild, uncoordinated running. A suicidal move if ever there was one.

"Don't kill him!" the medsys shouted again. "Let me sedate him. His condition is treatable." And with that, the medsys dove at the man in a smooth arc that passed over the top of the circle of death and struck the man in the butt with a hypodermic needle.

The man jumped, convulsively; and the medsys floated up, out of reach above his head. The circle widened to twice its original width but did not slow. The man's eyes calmed slightly; he wavered in his stance; then he fell to the ground on his side.

The black circle slowed, then stopped.

"Doctor Tolman," said the medsys, as it drifted low over the dirty, ragged, unconscious man, "I'd like you to meet Doctor Stanley Brewer—a member of the survey team. His main symptom is that he has remained constantly in a state of extreme fear."

Chapter 26

Lovely Dreams

Sammy woke slowly. He felt small, soft hands with long, stiff fingernails exploring his face and chest. A soothing voice whispered through the darkness. "Don't try to move or speak, you will be too groggy from the sedatives."

Sammy struggled to remember who he was and who this could be. He opened his mouth as though to speak through it, but of course used a com channel instead. "Barb?"

"Yesss," the voice cooed, "it's me, Barb. Now just lay still. Relax and enjoy."

The blanket flew away and the fingernails began to undress him. They worked swiftly, scratching the skin of his belly and legs several times.

Sammy strained to string words into sentences, "Need. . . cut your nails. They're. . . so long."

"Relax, my darling. Don't try to think. Let me think for us both."

Then he felt a weight on top of him. A soft, warm weight that conformed to his shape. It was at this point that he drifted back into a sleep-like state. Only this time there were dreams. Lovely wet-dreams.

Chapter 27

Pythagoras

Day 24

The next morning, Mark began looking for Tom. He had spent most of the previous evening and night trying to imagine better ways to communicate with the nano-robots. Ways that would allow him to convey more detailed information and more sophisticated ideas; hopefully to give them instructions, or even ask them questions.

Mark walked into Zebra's dining room and found Tom seated at one of the tables preparing to eat a large steaming plate of flat noodles covered with white sauce. Mark recognized this as chicken fettuccini alfredo. Not a remarkable thing in itself, and yet seeing it caused him to stop in mid-stride.

Tom noticed, and asked what was wrong.

Mark explained that he'd just realized he hadn't eaten in over a week. But more importantly, he hadn't even noticed that he hadn't eaten.

He checked with Blair to see if her eating habits had changed, and got similar results. Tom on the other hand had been eating steadily; and—as Blair was quick to point out—without gaining an ounce. But, of course, Tom's new eating habits existed only because hunger was one of his symptoms.

Mark theorized that their artificial bodies probably didn't need to ingest any food at all. But he also decided it was probably a good idea to eat at least a little something; and to do it regularly, just to make sure the nano-robots had all the material they might need to properly maintain their artificial human bodies. Mark resolved to join Tom for one meal in Zebra's dining room everyday; beginning immediately.

As Tom was finishing, with obvious joy, his chicken fettuccini alfredo, Mark stirred a small bowl of cream of mushroom soup. For years, this had been one of Mark's favorite dishes; and yet—though the soup was now cool enough to eat—he seemed to be having a little trouble working up the enthusiasm needed to lift a single spoonful to his mouth.

He paused from his stirring, rather abruptly; and began to stare at something on Tom's face.

Again Tom noticed the peculiar behavior. "Now what's the matter?" he asked, without bothering to clear his mouth of noodles or even slow his chewing.

"You have a new tattoo. On your cheek this time. The cheek with no bandage."

Tom frowned slightly. "Show me."

The image from Mark's eyes displayed a tired looking old man with three large squares drawn on his cheek. Each square had a grid-work of lesser squares inside it which plainly displayed the larger square's surface area. One large square measured 3X3, one 4X4, and one 5X5. The three large squares huddled so close together that two of each one's corners touched, and the empty space in the middle of the three formed a triangle. The differences in their sizes caused the two smaller squares to be placed at right angles to one another, and the largest to be placed diagonally.

Tom froze stiff as a statue and dropped his fork. It clanged on the table, but he didn't look at it. Slowly, he raised both hands to his face. He touched the tattoo as if to test if the squares were real. He stretched the skin this way and that; at first gently, but then with increasing roughness.

Mark saw the fear growing in Tom's eyes. "Relax, Tom. I really think you're overreacting."

"They've tapped into my memories! They can read my thoughts!"

"What are you talking about?"

"They know about the science club at my old college!"

"What?"

Tom stabbed at the new tattoo with an index finger. "That's the symbol of the University of Illinois, Science Club!"

Mark looked surprised at first, but then smiled and even laughed.

Tom's eyes flared. "You think this is funny?"

"Sorry, Tom. I can't help it. But you can relax; they aren't reading your memories. I remember those squares from college too. They're a graphical representation of the Pythagorean Theorem." Mark patted Tom on the back with a smile. "It's just as universal as Pi. It's the founding principal upon which all Trigonometry has been built. Those three squares demonstrate the relationship between a right triangle and the length of its hypotenuse: the diagonal line that lies opposite of the right angle. This relationship is built into the very structure of space. It's the same everywhere in the universe. Not really surprising that the nano-robots know about it."

"You're sure?"

Mark smiled. "Yesssssss." But his smile faded as his "sssss" stretched out long. His attention had been attracted to something on the table.

Tom followed Mark's gaze down to Tom's left arm, where he discovered that he had yet another new tattoo. A complicated arrangement of circles within circles.

"Medsys. Come here, please," said Tom. "I've got some new things to show you."

Two minutes later, the medsys floated into the room. Tom held out his left arm and turned his face to one side in order to present the tattoos for optimal viewing.

The medsys floated closer. "Fascinating! The Pythagorean Theorem. And... Hmmm. Those circles look rather like a... Just a moment. Let me confirm." A few seconds passed. "My guess was correct. I had to call Bonaparte to learn the orbital parameters of this star system's planets and moons. Those circles are a map of this solar system."

"The nano-robots understand astronomy?" asked Mark.

"It would appear so."

"Then the first tattoo could also be a map."

"Just a moment."

Tom and Mark glanced at each other.

"You are correct, Doctor," said the medsys. "It is a topological map of this planet. It details all the land masses and their primary river systems."

Chapter 28

Revenge of the Mad-Woman

While examining Tom's new tattoos, neither Tom, nor Mark, nor the medsys noticed a face peeping at them from around one of the large forest trees not far from Zebra. That face—its skin smeared with dirt, its eyes narrowed in anger—studied them remotely, through Zebra's open door.

"Fools!" the mad-woman whispered, actually speaking the words into the air with her mouth. "I'll teach them to mess with me!"

She worked her way from tree trunk to tree trunk, slowly, stealthfully.

"Who goes there?" asked the voice of the ambulance's comsys when she stepped inside it and closed its door behind her.

"It's only me," she whispered, just before smashing a series of three-inch-deep holes in the wall with a hammer where she estimated the comsys's tiny electronic brain should be. She'd beaten more than a dozen holes before she stopped to listen.

Holding her breath to deepen the silence, she cocked her head first one way and then another, but was unable to hear anyone running toward her. *If the machine had called out for help,* she reasoned, *they should have been here by now.* She stepped back to the door and peeked out.

From this location she could see only the area around Zebra's rear loading doors. It was deserted. "Good. The fools must still be inside Zebra, looking at the white-haired man's arms."

After easing the door shut, she dropped herself into the pilot seat at the control console, quickly read over the control labels, and grasped the joystick in her right hand. She smiled. "Looks simple enough."

She slid a throttle forward and was terrified to feel a surge of gee-force as the pilot seat shoved her body straight up into the sky. The ambulance, with her inside, was airborne.

The unexpected sensation threw her into a panic. She grabbed the edge of the control console with both hands to brace herself, but then just as quickly realized what must have happened and felt silly that she'd allowed herself to display such fear.

It was simple: the electronic gravity generators had not compensated for the craft's vertical acceleration. So her hammer blows—in addition to destroying the comsys—must have smashed their power source, or regulators, or something.

She shrugged off the fear, and again grabbed the joystick.

"I need a target."

She looked out the front window but saw only blue sky and a lumpy carpet of red tree-tops that extended to the horizon. She stretched her neck to see objects on the ground, especially those within the clearing below. She looked down upon Zebra. "Maybe that lander. Most of the fools seem to be living in it now."

Before she could make up her mind, however, a fast-moving black object smashed through one of the ambulance's side walls and fired a short burst of machine-gun bullets at her.

PLAGUE AT REDHOOK

She felt most of them enter her chest. The pain was sharp and deep, like being pierced by a cluster of arrows.

She tried to dodge any further bullets, but in doing so yanked and twisted the joystick. The ambulance responded with what might have looked to an outside observer as evasive maneuvers. From her perspective it appeared as though the small craft was trying to beat her to death with its walls and furniture. She bounced from wall to wall without releasing her grip on the joystick. At one point the black object crashed out through a side window, only to ram its way back in through the ceiling.

She swung her hammer at it, but the muscles of her arm were far too slow. The assault robot dodged easily. She swung again, and missed again. But this time the hammer's head buried itself inside the wall.

It must have hit something important. A huge ball of gas exploded from the wall and flashed a brilliant red. The fireball filled the craft, and swallowed her alive, giving her the sensation of being brutally punched everywhere on her body's surface, simultaneously. She then heard breaking glass, and felt the heat; intense heat that raced over all her skin, but especially inside her nose and mouth and across her eyes.

She screamed. Screamed like an animal being burned alive. But just as suddenly as it appeared, the heat and red brilliance vanished.

She fumbled for the craft's controls and tried to pull herself closer to the front window. Her vision was blurry; everything was surrounded by a fuzzy halo. The red fireball must have singed the lenses of her eyes.

She noticed a foul and puzzling smell. Puzzling, in that she'd smelled it before, but couldn't quite place it now. Then she recognized it; and immediately dismissed it as unimportant. It was just the smell of burnt hair. Hers.

She glanced about inside the craft for the black object that had attacked her. The ambulance's previously white interior was now burned various shades of brown and tan. The windows were all broken—blown out by the fireball. And her flying enemy was gone.

Through the now glass-less front window, she strained to spot a worthy target. "There!" She smiled, and felt her seared lips crack open in several places. The cracking was painful, but still she did not care. "People!"

Down below, two men stood together on the red grass outside Zebra, accompanied by a floating medsys. They stared up at her. Their mouths were open. One—the old white-haired man—was pointing at her.

"The fools."

She tilted the joystick toward them, aiming the craft for one last suicidal dive.

A beam of pure blue light sliced upward through the floor and instantly burned its way through the ceiling. She glanced at it long enough to see it begin winding a jagged path through the craft's cabin toward her. She recognized it as another of the assault robot's weapons, and knew her enemy would not make the mistake of entering the craft again.

"Got to hurry!" she mumbled. "No time to dodge. Got to kill them fast!"

The blue laser beam bit into her left forearm. She jumped up onto the console to buy herself a few extra seconds of revenge. She didn't notice her left hand hit the floor.

A second blue beam entered through one of the walls. Then a third came in through the ceiling. They had her surrounded. Still she didn't care. The craft was heading straight for the fools. She smiled, and felt more cracking. She licked her lips, tasting the fresh blood as she smeared it about.

Through the front window, she could see the blurry people down there bumping into one another, trying to run away. She laughed, maniacally; hoping it was loud enough to be heard on the ground.

A blue beam caught her shoulder. She tried to duck, but in doing so stepped on the joystick; and before realizing, had shifted onto it her full weight.

Chapter 29

Crash Landing

At that very moment, Tom lifted his face and chest from the ground and spat red blades of grass from his mouth. He jerked his head up and looked at the ambulance in the sky. It was spinning now. Spinning like a gigantic child's toy. He was about to get up and start running again when his frantic brain recalculated the craft's trajectory. It was no longer coming at him. It was now gaining altitude.

The spinning craft rose a hundred feet, then slowly turned upside down and fell screaming out of the sky. Literally screaming. Either the craft itself was producing the hideous high pitched wail, or someone inside it.

The ambulance crashed onto Gemsbok. But it was no simple impact crash; it was a spinning, grinding, flailing crash. A crash that threw great chucks of furniture and strips of metal hundreds of feet in every direction.

Tom—three hundred feet away—watched as some of the larger objects bounced and rolled before floundering to a stop.

Stephen Euin Cobb

But while most of these objects were still in motion, hundreds of smaller objects, mostly unidentifiable fragments of hard plastic, glass and ceramic, began raining out of the sky onto the grass all around him. Half a dozen such items struck his hair and chest and legs. He first squinted at the harsh little impacts, then covered his eyes with a tattooed forearm.

This false rain lasted no more than a second or two. When he lowered his arm, he spotted two heavy white chairs tumbling down out of the sky—one straight at him. Each had a single metal leg which ended in a jagged stump where it had been torn loose from the ambulance's floor.

He half-crawled half-jumped aside, and felt the soil quake as they slammed into the nearby ground. He saw one of the chairs fly up, then over his head, flipping end over end. It hit the ground a second time and began rolling wildly. It finally flopped onto its back, and slid an additional thirty feet.

With this immediate danger past, Tom rolled over, sat up, and banged the back of his head against the seat of the other chair. It was standing upright, leaning only slightly, and spinning on its swivel. Its one metal leg had stabbed deep into the grass, like a dart into a dartboard. He tried not to think how it would have been if, instead, it had stabbed into his chest.

He slowed its spinning to a stop, and used it to pull himself up onto his feet. He then hurried to the crash site. Mark and the medsys were already there.

Gemsbok was a total loss. The mad-woman had undoubtedly killed all the sleepers it housed. That is, in addition to herself.

Tom spotted a disembodied hand laying on the grass. It was a man's hand, severed cleanly at the wrist. He felt his stomach wretch and had to turn away. It was a full minute before he was able to turn back.

Chapter 30

Find Her!

Mark ran his fingers through his black hair as he walked around the edge of the wreckage, searching for something that resembled human bodies—or parts thereof. He noticed Tom dutifully scanning the wreckage too, but it was clear from the look on the old man's face that he was hoping he wouldn't spot anything. The captain looked as though he might throw-up at any moment.

Mark understood. He felt queasy in his stomach too, but not because of the gore. Blood and guts and miscellaneous body parts didn't bother him. No, for him it was the massive loss of life. *Such a waste. Loss of life is always such a. . .* Mark stopped walking. He froze in mid-stride with a look of fear on his face. *Good Lord in heaven! How could I have been so stupid!*

Mark climbed up into the tangled wreckage. "Medsys! Tom! Help me!" He shoved large pieces of debris out of his way to search behind them.

Tom hurried to where Mark had stood, almost bumping into the approaching medsys. "What's wrong?"

"We have to find whatever's left of the mad-woman! The pieces of her. All of them!"

"Why?" Tom asked, openly confused.

"Because the nano-robots may try to rebuild her. No, I take that back. Not may, they will try. And if they do, they'll probably make one of her out of each piece. And if they succeed, we might have to face ten of her next time; and every one of those ten would be just as suicidally crazy as this one was!"

Tom fumbled through a thousand disconnected thoughts trying to formulate a single sentence. He failed, then failed, then failed again.

"Rebuild her?" said the medsys. "Are you insane?"

Mark glanced at the medsys, then at Tom. "Take my word for it. It's important. If you can't believe me. . . Well then. . . Well then. . ." He looked around as though searching for an explanation. He finally gave up and shrugged wildly in desperation. "Humor me!"

Chapter 31

Euthanasia

Dorothy Ponder lay on her bed in the dark. Though there was nothing to see, her eyes were open. She was unable to sleep. This wasn't a plague symptom. It was worry. She was having second thoughts. *What if I'm told to nuke the planet and kill everyone down there? Should I obey such an order? Am I even capable of it?*

She sat up and turned enough to drop her legs over the edge of the bed. She spoke into the darkness. "PC?"

A voice responded from atop her desk. "Yes, commander?"

"What is the minimum response time for a message torpedo to Fort Delk?"

"Round trip to Big Sandy at zero point eight eight light-years per day, is six point one days."

"Thank you."

She laid back down; eyes still open. *Five days to go. Five days before I'll know the verdict.* She rolled over and faced the wall. *Will it be murder? Or will they call it euthanasia?*

Chapter 32

Half-Man

Mark reached down, got a good grip on a collapsed section of wall, glanced at Tom to make sure he had a good grip too, and shouted, "One. Two. Three!" The two men strained until the section of wall stood vertical. It then shifted slightly, as a portion of its bottom edge crumbled under the weight.

"Now, push!" Mark added. They shoved it hard enough to make it fall slowly away from them, crashing onto its back.

Mark had managed to talk Tom into helping him move some of the larger pieces of wreckage, but only after he'd carefully cleared the area of all visible body parts.

The medsys approached, and said softly, "Doctor, may I speak with you."

"Sure, go ahead."

"I mean privately."

Mark's mouth was open, and he was breathing heavily, two things which wouldn't alter his voice through the link; still his tone carried a small amount of annoyance. "Can't you just switch to one of the medical channels?"

PLAGUE AT REDHOOK

Surely, Mark thought, he needn't explain to a medsys that, like military and government channels, the medical com channels were not accessible to standard PC users—Tom, for example.

"I intend to," said the machine, "but privately."

Mark looked at Tom with a shrug, "Excuse me."

As the medsys lead Mark away from the wreckage, toward the lander Zebra, it changed to a medical channel and said, "A patient is asking for you."

"So what? Can't you handle it?"

"It's Doctor Williams."

Mark stopped in his tracks. "The—" He glanced around: a useless gesture in an age of radio thought-links. He'd almost said, *The hand!* He turned to the machine and thought softly. "His head is complete?"

"No. His face is. Well, mostly. But the point is he's conscious and wants to know what's going on."

"He can speak?"

"Yes."

"Does he remember the explosion? Or being hurt?"

"He—"

"Does he know that he's. . . incomplete?"

"Well. . ."

Mark didn't wait for an answer. He took off running toward Zebra, leaving the medsys to catch up. He trotted into the bio-lab to find Doctor Williams, still laying on the blanket on the floor behind the lab bench where he'd been placed more than three weeks ago. Only now he was awake. Awake and wrestling.

Blair was sitting on his chest, her knees on the blanket at his sides. Both her hands squeezed his solitary wrist, trying unsuccessfully to keep his one arm from flailing about.

"Let me up young woman!" He yelled with his mouth, spitting and sputtering as he did so. "I demand to know what's going on around here. I want to see a doctor!"

Stephen Euin Cobb

Half of the man's cranium was missing. It looked as though it had been sliced off at an odd angle just above the eyes by a clumsy guillotine operator. Most of his chest was complete, but his other shoulder and arm were still missing; as was all of his body from the lower ribs down.

"Doctor Williams, please relax," said Mark—automatically using one of the lower com channels, despite the patient's use of his mouth. "I am your doctor."

"Well, it's about time," said the unfinished man using the same com channel. And with that he reduced the fierceness of his wrestling—though his vocalizations remained as violent. "Why am I being held here against my will? And why is my PC not working properly? I can't log onto the public net at all, and half the com channels are garbled beyond recognition!"

"I'll answer all your questions shortly, but I must first learn just how you are faring. Are you in any pain? Do you feel any discomfort?"

"Except for this woman sitting on my chest, I'm fine, thank you. Now if you please—"

"Are you aware. . .?" Mark started. But Blair shook her head vigorously; her eyes large and urgent. Mark paused; then frowned. "He doesn't know?"

"No!" she said.

Mark tilted his head to one side. "He hasn't seen himself?"

Her eyes grew even larger. She gritted her teeth. "No!"

Mark turned to the medsys. "Sedate him."

"I don't know what?" Doctor Williams said.

"But he says he's fine," the medsys protested.

Mark shook his head. "I don't care. Do it."

Doctor Williams thrashed under Blair's weight, shaking her violently from side to side. She then rose and fell like a cowgirl riding a bronco in a wild west rodeo. "I haven't seen what?" he shouted through his mouth.

The medsys still hesitated. "But, he—"

Mark drew his fist back, threatening to strike the floating machine. "Do it! Now!"

Chapter 33

People Puzzles

Day 29

It had taken five days to find and gather what seemed to be all the body parts strewn through the wreckage. Doing the job properly had required moving all the fragmentary remains of the destroyed ambulance and lander to a new spot about seventy feet away from the crash site.

Tom had helped as long as he could, but on the very first day the task became too grisly for him to stomach. Blair lasted a few hours longer than Tom, but after she found her first head—or to be more accurate her first half of a head; its one eye gently shut in slumber and air softly, if mysteriously, entering and exiting its nostrils; nostrils which, it should be mentioned, were not attached to any lungs—she too found herself involuntarily bowing out. And both the bowing and the involuntarily were literal. She dry-heaved for three full minutes.

Mark and the medsys had worked on tirelessly; one because machines don't get tired, the other because tirelessness was one of his plague symptoms.

The two of them laid out the mostly inanimate body parts in the red grass; the bright sun shining on them all.

During the search, Mark had secretly watched for a hand—or anything else for that matter—to grope its way out of the wreckage. But none of the parts manifested any motion other than breathing.

It was not one of the sleeper's body parts that Mark expected to show dramatic movement, but those of the madwoman. At first he'd kept a special eye out for parts with burned skin; but when none were found, he soon decided the nano-robots had probably repaired her burn damage within minutes.

For a time, Mark theorized that the nano-robots had accidentally changed her appearance as they repaired her, but he couldn't convince himself that this would prove true.

Finally, he began discovering pieces that were verifiably hers. And by this time, he had worked out a plan of action. Each time he located some new piece of her, he immediately sedated it, and placed it together with her other parts. If they suddenly became animated, at least they would be sluggish and disoriented as they tried to create mischief.

Repeatedly, he found himself wondering why the sedatives worked at all. His best guess was that the nano-robots had at some point observed normal organic tissues reacting to the chemical sedatives, and so now monitored the blood for such chemicals; and when those chemicals were detected, the little robots then changed the behavior of the artificial cells to match what they had observed. Mark had no evidence to support this theory, but it made a whole lot more sense than pretending that the same compounds that will sedate an organic human will, just naturally, sedate an artificial one as well.

"This goes here," Mark said, walking amidst a hundred body parts strewn about the grass. He set the foot he was carrying at the end of a leg, which was itself next to another leg and most of a torso, though there was no associated head. "And I think this hand goes with that arm over there."

"Yes, I think you're right," said the medsys. "And that leg goes there."

They were sorting through the parts they'd found; trying to put the human jigsaw puzzles back together. They were doing well so far, but they both knew they were going to run into problems once they tried to pass out the pile of heads. Each limb and torso had been broken or ripped or severed in a slightly different location, which provided small clues as to where it had originated. But most of the heads had simply come off at the neck, which meant they'd all come loose at almost the same place, in almost the same way.

Still, Mark wasn't ready to give up. Not yet.

"This hand probably goes here," he said. "And this probably. . ." He stopped and stood very still. He shook his head and blinked a couple of times. Then he said, "Wasn't that hand severed?"

"Which one?"

"That one." He pointed to a hand that was clearly not severed, but attached seamlessly to a disembodied arm.

The medsys replayed some of its digitally stored memory images. "You are correct. That hand was severed at the wrist when you placed it at the end of that arm. The nano-robots must have reattached it while we were occupied elsewhere."

Mark felt a chill of fear at first, but then smiled slightly. He leaned back and laughed out loud.

The medsys hurried to his side. "Why are you laughing? Are you all right"

"How could I have been so stupid?"

"I don't understand."

Mark spun around and waved his hands at the field of body parts. "How many parts have rejoined themselves?"

The medsys checked its visual memory. "I count eighteen."

"And how many parts have not rejoined themselves? Twenty? Twenty-five?"

"I count thirty-two."

Mark slapped his hands together and laughed again. "This is going to be easy!" He grabbed up a head in each hand and placed one in contact with the severed neck at the top of each of two torsos. He then hurried back and grabbed two more heads, which he placed at the top of two other torsos. Once finished with heads he began placing arms and hands and feet in their respective positions but without any apparent regard for whose body they actually belonged to.

"What are you doing?" asked the medsys. "That hand doesn't go there, it has too much attached forearm. And that's a woman's body. You've given it a head with a beard!"

Mark just smiled and continued passing out body parts. When he ran out of parts he sat down in the red grass at the base of a tree. He leaned back with a smile and put his hands behind his head.

The medsys floated closer to him. "Most of what you have just done is wrong."

"I know."

"Then why did you do it?"

"Because it's easier than wracking my brain trying to figure out what's right."

"I don't understand."

"I know." He grinned. "That's the funny part."

"Then perhaps you would like to enlighten me."

Mark laughed one more time, then leaned forward. "OK, OK. In five or ten minutes I'll get up from this spot and move all the parts that have not joined themselves together, to new locations. Then I'll wait another ten minutes and move those that are still not joined. And I'll keep doing it every ten minutes for as long as it takes for all the parts to become joined to their proper bodies."

"Of course," the machine said. "I see."

Mark leaned back, still smiling. "Exactly. Why should I worry about it? The nano-robots know which parts go with which bodies; the proof is that they refused to connect improper parts even when I placed them in direct contact." Again, he put his hands behind his head and leaned back against the tree. "Yep," he said, "this is going to be easy."

Chapter 34

Naked Sleepers & Children's Writing

A few hours later, in Zebra's dining room, Tom gripped the white padded armrests of his favorite easy chair. "OK, I'm ready." He held very still; so much so that, without realizing it, he was holding his breath.

"Please, try to relax," the medsys said. "You don't have to become a statue for this."

"I'm just a little nervous."

"You won't feel a thing."

"I know that," Tom said as though insulted. "I'm nervous about the result."

"Ditto," Mark said with emphasis. He gave Tom a smile of encouragement.

Tom managed only half a smile in return, then looked at the medsys and said, "Let's do it."

The medsys floated closer to Tom's chest. "I am beginning now." And with that, the machine began to send pulses of broadband radio waves straight into Tom's chest. The pulses formed a complicated string of meaningless random numbers.

PLAGUE AT REDHOOK

The logic behind this little experiment was simple. When the nano-robots had reconstructed the head of Doctor Williams, they somehow gave it the ability to perform—in a highly imperfect way—some of the communication functions of a PC. Doctor Williams was clearly able to send and receive his audio-thoughts on at least one com channel, yet his head contained no PC. Not one of human manufacture; and not one of any alien design that Mark could locate using X-rays, ultrasound, or the several other penetrating scanners which he regularly used to examine people's insides. This suggested that it was the nano-robots themselves—those composing Doctor Williams' head or body—that were sending and receiving the information encoded in radio waves.

Most of the frequencies the medsys was using for this experiment were the same ones used for thought-link com channels. Except that the com channels were all digital, all filtered, and all frequency modulated on carrier waves of approximately uniform amplitude. For this, the medsys was instead using amplitude modulation—the old AM, rather than the newer FM. Consequently, the humans heard nothing through the link.

Tom looked at the medsys; then up at Mark—who was standing, perhaps too nervous to sit—then back to the machine.

After twelve seconds the medsys announced, "Broadcast is complete." It floated away from Tom's chest, and took a position next to Mark. "Now all we can do is wait."

The three waited in silence for several minutes, but as the minutes stretched out, they began to talk. Tom was curious about the mad-woman. Mark described how he'd sedated each piece of her as it had been located; and how her almost fully reconstituted body was now safely unconscious in Zebra's bio-lab. He had refilled her medcom, which he'd found empty of sedatives. But out of fear that it might have been damaged in the crash, he was administering her current series of sedatives himself, by-hand, every twelve hours.

Blair entered Zebra through the side door with a confused look on her face. "Mark, I was just in Elk," she said. "Checking on its sleepers. Did you. . . ?" She blinked and shook her head as if trying to emphasize her confusion. "Did you undress some of them?"

"Undress them?" Now Mark looked confused. He shook his head slowly and said, "No."

"Well two of the male sleepers are completely naked."

"Naked?"

"Yeah. And that woman you brought back from the star shuttle. She's not in her bed."

"What?" Mark nearly bumped into the medsys trying to get closer to Blair. "She's gone? Are you sure?"

"You can look for yourself, if you want. But I couldn't find her. I figured you must have taken her off sedation."

"Damn!" Mark made a fist, and stared intently out Zebra's side door. "I haven't checked on her in days. Her medcom must have run out of sedatives." He strode to the door and glanced around at the horizon—what little he could see of it. "She could be anywhere by now. There's no telling how long she's been awake. She must have made love to them while they slept."

"What?" Blair said, visibly shocked. "Is she crazy?"

Tom decided, despite his shame, that it was time for him to admit to his little encounter with the mystery woman. "I—"

"There it is!" the medsys shouted. "They did it!" The machine swooped in just inches from Tom's chest. It moved so fast that Tom jerked back and might have flipped his chair over, if it hadn't been attached to the floor.

"What's all the excitement?" Blair asked.

"I sent radio pulses into Tom's chest a few minutes ago," the medsys said, "and now his chest has sent identical radio pulses back."

"You're kidding," she said, and sounded like she meant it.

"No," answered the machine. "Tom, I am now going to try broadcasting a more complicated pattern of pulses, using a narrower frequency range."

Tom nodded. "Fire when ready."

"Transmission is compleeeee—They are returning it already."

Mark slapped his hands together, and danced some kind of little jig. He then stopped abruptly. "Try sending a musical series," he suggested.

"As you wish."

Everyone watched the medsys in silence.

"And they are returning it now," said the machine. "Exactly as I sent it."

Mark paced. "We need something more complicated. A real quantum leap."

"Video," said Blair with a shrug.

Mark pointed at her. "Exactly!"

"That may be a difficult leap for them, but it is a logical step," said the medsys. "I'll start with a single frame; a still picture as it were."

Five seconds later, Tom's entire forehead was covered by Leonardo da Vinci's famous painting of The Last Supper. The top of the painting extended just above Tom's hairline, so some of its details were obscured by white hair.

Mark and Blair's mouths both dropped open. Tom's mouth joined theirs when he spotted it through Mark's eyes.

The medsys droned, "Image return, successful."

Of the three humans, Mark recovered first. He laughed; loud and long.

"I am now transmitting a series of moving images and linguistic data," said the medsys. "I have no idea how extensive a sample they will need in order to sort through this material and make sense of it. All I can do is give them a steady stream and hope for the best. I may only be confusing the heck out of them."

Mark asked, "What are you sending?"

"A video encyclopedia."

He frowned. "Don't you think that'll be too complicated for them?"

"It might be. I hope not. This encyclopedia was created for small children."

Mark bit his lip.

Seconds passed in silence.

"Transmission complete. Awaiting reply."

Mark stared at Tom's chest, then glanced up at the painting on his forehead. It was unchanged. He looked at Blair, she was staring at the medsys, waiting for it to announce a response.

Tom cleared his throat.

Mark swallowed hard. The tension was getting thick. He smiled for a moment, imagining how one big sneeze from Blair would probably send them all jumping.

He didn't realize it at first, but the image on Tom's forehead was slowly fading back to its normal skin color. He noticed just before it was completely gone.

Then, as if written by an invisible hand, two words appeared in its place. The words were written letter-by-letter in that clumsy irregular style that artists often use when trying to mimic the writing of small children. The two words were: "We understand."

Chapter 35

Nuke 'Em Till They Glow

"Incoming torpedo," Lieutenant alpha announced.

"Reception procedures initiated," chanted Lieutenant sigma.

The commander stood from her chair. "I'll take it in my quarters." She turned and walked off the bridge.

Inside her small apartment, she closed the door and proceeded to her desk. Before she could even seat herself, a shiny metal cylinder—twelve inches long and three inches wide—slid out of a little round hole in the wall and dropped into a shallow trough molded into the left edge of her desk.

She took her seat and raised a hand to reach for the cylinder, but just before touching it, she stopped. An unfamiliar wave of fear washed over her body. Fear at what decisions and orders this torpedo might contain.

Her duty and oaths would require that she execute them, no matter how repugnant she found them personally. There were limits, of course. Officially she could refuse any order, provided she was certain it was illegal, or unconscionable, or if she could convincingly assert that it was contrary to her religious convictions. Officially.

In actual practice—as far as she understood it—people did not reach her exalted rank in SpaceGuard by respectfully refusing to carry out orders just when the going got ugly.

For a number of seconds she watched the shiny object roll from side-to-side in the trough. Then, in a fit of determination, she snatched it up, unscrewed one end, and from its mostly hollow interior, removed a fat wad of padding composed of a single sheet of softly foamed plastic. She spent almost a full minute unwrapping its many protective layers before locating the tiny message chip cradled gently inside.

It did not occur to her to wonder why everyone called these things chips when they actually resembled clear glass cubes. At some point in her formal education, she had probably been told that just over a century ago, before computers had become fully optical (with their fiber-optic light-guides and solid state microlasers) they had been composed entirely of electrical circuits contained on tiny silicon chips. But even if she had wondered about it now, she probably wouldn't have cared. Instead, without so much as a second thought, she plugged it into her handheld computer, told the machine the proper decipher code, and read the results.

She raised an eyebrow.

Apparently SpaceGuard was taking this quarantine seriously. This torpedo was from Vice Admiral Victor Santos—three ranks above her, and the highest ranking officer at Big Sandy's Fort Delk. To reach anyone higher she would have had to send a torpedo all the way to Earth; a distance of seventy light-years, and an eighty day trip one way—a hundred and sixty days if you were waiting for a reply.

For convenience, someone within the military had assigned planet E-33 a name: Redhook. Commander Ponder recognized it as the name of a small town in North America.

PLAGUE AT REDHOOK

The Admiral, after studying all the information provided—or so he said—had issued her three specific orders.

[1] Until further notice, the situation at Redhook was to be kept a military secret. This would be a total information blackout. No message torpedoes were to leave Redhook's star system unless they were sent directly to the Admiral himself.

[2] She, Commander Ponder, shall continue to maintain the quarantine—using lethal force, if necessary—until everyone on Redhook is dead; either of old age, or of the disease.

She frowned, slightly. *Or of the enforcement?*

The Admiral explained that nine warships were being diverted from their various patrol areas to rendezvous with her at Redhook: two carriers, four cutters, and three caravels. When their arsenals were combined with that of Bonaparte, they would provide over four hundred carbon-fusion warheads that can be deployed against the surface. This will allow her to carry out the third and final order.

[3] After all are dead, the planet's surface is to be nuked into oblivion.

She nodded at this last one—though unsure if she were nodding agreement with the decision, or just that she understood it. She managed a weak smile. "At least the only civilians I'll have to kill are those who try to leave the planet." She leaned back and looked at the burnished metal ceiling. Her weak smile faded. When it was gone, she said, "May that number be small."

Chapter 36

Visible Change

Still in the easy chair in Zebra's dining room, Tom glanced from the medsys, hovering in front of him, to Mark and then to Blair, who flanked the spherical floating robot. "OK." Tom nodded. "Do it."

"As you wish," said the medsys, and it began transmitting into Tom's chest all the medical data it possessed concerning the normal functioning of a healthy human body. This was a considerable quantity of knowledge; one that it had announced would require one hundred and forty-seven minutes to transmit.

Tom felt an odd tingling of terror crawl up his spine and a cold sweat spread slowly across his chest. It had just occurred to him that by giving the nano-robots a complete understanding of how the human body operates they will now be able to more effectively torment us.

He looked up at Mark for some kind of reassurance that they were doing the right thing, but Mark just stared at Tom's chest. Tom looked at Blair, then at the medsys. He shifted uncomfortably in his seat.

PLAGUE AT REDHOOK

After a few more minutes—and long before the medsys's transmission would be complete—he decided quite suddenly that something was wrong; very very wrong. But he had no idea what it might be. He looked at Blair again, squinting this time.

Her face. Something different about her face.

Then he got it. The skin was now an ordinary shade of tan which blended naturally with the rest of her face. The redness around her eyes and nostrils was gone.

"Blair," he said, "your eyes aren't red!"

But before she could respond, Tom's mind was crowded with voices. Dozens of people, both men and women, clogged the lower thought-link channels with hundreds of overlapping statements. Some whined and complained, but most just sounded confused.

The sleepers! They're awake!

Tom poked his stomach just below the ribs with his fingertips. He frowned. *I'm still hungry.* He poked his stomach again, but this time just below the navel. He smiled. *But I don't need to pee!*

He reached a hand up to his cheek and peeled off the thick gauze bandage. He began feeling around for the cut that had never stopped bleeding.

He couldn't find it.

Chapter 37

Exile

The commander swiveled slightly as she leaned forward in her black command chair. "All the symptoms? You're sure?"

"Yes," Mark said. "I've checked everyone. Apparently the nano-robotic group-mind occupying Captain Vickery's body digested the medical information and transmitted it to the group-minds occupying the other nano-humans. Everyone's symptoms disappeared at approximately the same time."

Mark added, quickly, "Except those of Doctor Williams of course. He's still physically incomplete. I'll take him off sedation as soon as his body is whole. A week and a half, at most."

"That's wonderful, Doctor," she said with obvious sincerity. "I will convey this new information to SpaceGuard Regional Command at once."

She hesitated for a moment. Her countenance clouded, and she blinked nervously a few times before continuing. "I must warn you, however, that there is a good chance my superiors

PLAGUE AT REDHOOK

will insist the quarantine remain in place. That is, at least for a period sufficient to observe the more long-term effects."

She blinked twice more. "After all, even if appearing perfectly healthy, your bodies remain artificial; filled with millions of nano-robots. Technically, you are all highly contagious."

She paused again, very briefly. "I just don't want any of the people down there to get their hopes up; to begin thinking that since everyone seems healthy, suddenly everyone can go home. In my opinion, that is not likely."

Mark frowned. "How long might this take?"

"I'm not a Doctor," she said, without intending any sarcasm; and had to fight to keep herself from apologizing for the slip. "But if I were guessing, I might say a year. Maybe less," she added quickly. But then had to follow with: "maybe more."

Secretly, she thought: *Or maybe the rest of your lives.*

"You see," she said softly, almost gently, "it's not at all proven that the nano-robots mean you no harm. Only time can show that with any assurance."

Mark looked down. His voice devoid of the excitement it had possessed when he'd started this conversation. "I see."

"Do not give up hope, Doctor," she said crisply, trying to sound chipper. "I will convey this new information, and we will see what decisions come back. In the meantime I think we need to make everyone down there as comfortable as possible. I'll send for more spacious living quarters that can be dropped to you from orbit inside expendable re-entry craft, then parachuted to the ground. I'll also arrange to send down a few dozen cleaning robots; more and better food rations; as well as the general day-to-day needs of a civilized people."

She had hoped this would cheer him, but it didn't seem to be working. She wasn't surprised. While it wasn't exactly Siberia, she had just told him that he was to remain in exile. And that there was no telling how long his exile might last.

She made another attempt: "Please make a list of everyone's special needs and personal preferences concerning entertainment programs, movies, books and music. You might also check to see if anyone has hobbies with which they would like to occupy themselves. I can probably provide you with pretty much anything. . . within reason."

Chapter 38

Free Stuff

"We can have stuff for free?" asked Blair.

"I guess so." Mark shrugged; then took a seat at Zebra's dining table. "She didn't say anything about us paying for anything."

"Well, if it's free, I could sure use some new clothes."

"I don't think you understand," Mark scolded. "We are going to be kept here like prisoners. Maybe for years. Maybe forever!"

Blair frowned at him. "We have a big beautiful planet to live on, and all the free stuff we want? Sounds like my kind of prison."

From an easy chair, Tom said, "Mark, you look more worried about this than I am. Is there something you're not telling us?"

"I think she wants to keep us here."

"The commander?"

"Yes. I think she's afraid of us; or of what we've become."

Tom squinted. "Why?"

"I don't know. Or at least I'm not sure." Mark shook his head. "I don't know, maybe I'm being overly sensitive; reading too much into her tone and body language." He slapped the table top, and stood up. "I suppose we'd better call everyone together and let them know what's going on. Sort of a town meeting, I guess." He smiled. "Town is right. Soon we'll have enough houses down here to call it a town."

Chapter 39

Meeting

The meeting went poorly. It was repeatedly interrupted to explain to one individual, or group, all the things they had missed; either by being absent from an event or unconscious—by sedation or prolonged sleep.

The sleepers had the most questions; the undead were a close second. The passionate woman failed to attend, perhaps out of shame. The frightened man was able to provide some answers, but Doctor Williams and the mad-woman were both under sedation. Doctor Williams because he was still incomplete; the mad-woman because—though her body had been reassembled easily after the parts were located—most of her head was never found. It was presumed destroyed in the crash.

After talking with the undead, Mark was able to establish some of the events that lead up the explosion:

Raymond Hill—Andromeda's still missing passenger—for example, like the mad-woman, had developed some kind of terrible anger. He'd become infected while in a fit of rage over something; and once stuck in that emotional extreme, had expanded his rage to include the passengers and crew, and finally the ship itself.

Doctor Williams—at that point, already artificial and a nano-plague carrier—followed this mad-man to Andromeda's engine room and tried to stop his destructive actions. But when the doctor sounded an alarm to the crew, the mad-man took the doctor as hostage. The four crewmembers and all but one passenger gathered in the engine room, in an impromptu effort to rescue Doctor Williams. This was when the mad-man triggered the explosion.

Being at the explosion's center, the mad-man was completely destroyed—the artificial tissues of his body as well as the individual nano-robots maintaining him. Most of Doctor Williams' body was likewise destroyed; with the exception of one hand. The crew, and all those passengers present, died of impact damage.

Mark had theorized, previously, that the undead must have received their contamination at the instant Andromeda exploded. It was now apparent that this occurred when tiny fragments of the body of Doctor Williams exploded against their skin. These fragments contained countless individual nano-robots, which immediately started to work, replacing the organic cells that were nearest at hand—the cells of the skin of people who had died that very instant. Consequently, at the time of death, the skin of the undead were being replaced; while the tissues deeper inside their bodies were transformed in the minutes that followed.

Concerning the passionate woman's transformation, Mark could only guess. And what guesses he made, he kept to himself.

She must have been in a high state of erotic arousal at the moment her hypothalamus was replaced; but based upon the location of everyone else aboard Andromeda, Mark couldn't work out who she could possibly have been with.

PLAGUE AT REDHOOK

He decided never to ask her, even indirectly. And that, in all future conversation, he must avoid any possible hint that he suspected. Because, the only logical solution seemed to be that she had been alone, making love to herself.

But wait; she couldn't have been. If she'd been masturbating, she would have been locked into a state-of-mind that would have prompted her to continue self-stimulating. Not one that had her repeatedly seeking a male sex partner. She must have been in full coitus with a male when the tissue composing her hypothalamus was replaced.

What's more: either the sex act was never completed, or the hypothalamic replacement occurred just before her climax, thus locking her into that state of extreme arousal.

Odd that when I first contacted her she was so quick to plead; so quick to suggest bondage and spanking. This would make sense, of course, if she was the submissive partner in a submissive/dominant relationship.

But if there was a male, who could it have been? Could it have been the one person still missing? The one person who will never be able to tell his side of events? The mystery man: Raymond Hill? If so, he may have been with her only hours before the explosion destroyed the ship and ended his life.

Chapter 40

Guard Duty

Day 35

Six days later, seated at her desk, in the privacy of her quarters, Dorothy Ponder read the decoded message. It was just as she had expected. The sudden health of the plague sufferers had not altered her orders, or the decisions they were based upon. No one and nothing was to be allowed to leave Redhook's biosphere; and as soon as all the humans were dead, the biosphere was to be destroyed.

It was not only what she had expected, it was also what she'd wanted. Though now that she read it, she felt a pang of remorse, of sadness, perhaps even a shade of guilt.

Slowly, she reached out and turned off her computer. "My job now is to wait. To wait and to watch." She stood and walked to the door. "Glorified guard duty."

Chapter 41

Until The End

Perched atop his lab stool, Mark focused his attention on the image fed into his mind's eye by the electron microscope. Nano-robots streamed though artificial-living tissue like ants in an ant farm. Always moving, always working, never wasting time, never hesitating, never giving up. Why can't I be like that? he thought.

But he knew the answer, and the answer was bitter: He was like that. He was exactly like that. And now the work he loved was over. My profession—the field I slaved through twelve years to learn—is now just as useless as that of Touch-Typist.

But there was another dismal thought brewing in his troubled brain. Something he felt should have been a good thing; yet somehow he felt oddly doomed by it. As though he were in some kind of bizarre purgatory.

"Mark," said the medsys floating into the bio-lab behind him. "What's troubling you? You needn't deny it. I can tell something is wrong."

Mark sighed deeply. He turned on the stool to face the machine. "You haven't guessed it yet either?"

"Guessed what?"

"The nano-robots. Whoever made them, I mean. They did it so they could enjoy good health. They wanted a body that could repair itself if injured. One that was immune to all diseases."

"So, what's wrong with that?"

"Nothing." Mark shrugged. "It's great. As a doctor, I'm all for it. It's just that, in our civilization, being artificial— Well, it makes us all a bunch of freaks. What's worse, I keep getting the impression. . ." His voice faded away.

"What?"

"Well. . . I feel as though the military is planning to keep us all locked up here until we die."

"No offence, doctor, but there are worse places to die."

"But, that's just it," he blurted. "We're not going to!"

"Not going to what?" it asked calmly.

Mark leaned forward. "How stupid are you? Do you think for one minute that the nano-robots are going to sit down on their tiny little butts long enough to let us die? Billions of years from now Earth's sun will burn out and the oceans will all freeze over. And me and Tom and Blair and everybody else here will still be alive to see it!"

Chapter 42

The Town's Newest Citizen

The town wasn't very big as towns go, but with a population of only fifty-three it didn't need to be. Nearly finished, it still didn't have a name. Suggestions ran from Alcatraz to Utopia, with the obvious—if somewhat clumsy—possibilities of Nanoville, Nanoburg and Nanodelphia.

The heart of the town was a single paved street three hundred feet long, with a town hall at one end and a small multi-faith chapel at the other. Twenty houses on one side of the street, and twenty houses on the other, sheltered its tiny population. More would have been required if fewer of its residents had been married.

Construction robots had assembled all the partially prefabricated houses, and had paved the single road and network of sidewalks. Barb and Sammy had organized the construction robots and overseen their progress.

A long sidewalk ran past the chapel and down to the lake, which now had a small pier with two canoes and one power boat tied to it.

Stephen Euin Cobb

The landers, Zebra and Elk, sat on the red grassy field a few hundred feet outside of town. They and the lake and the town formed a triangle, surrounded by the great trees of red and yellow and brown.

In Zebra's dining room, Tom sat alone, reading an engineering journal suspended in the air before him. Its articles all related to his captainly duties. He was tense; waiting for the results of Mark's work in the bio-lab at the craft's other end.

Mark was still using Zebra's bio-lab for his research, and on this day at least—if perhaps never again—to dispense a little medical assistance.

"Next page," Tom though to his PC.

The journal's page turned.

Tom frowned. He'd been hoping that by reading about his job he might be able to convince himself that someday he would get off this planet. So far, it didn't seem to be working. "Next."

Another page turned.

A high pitched squeal escaped Zebra's laboratory. Tom flinched in alarm; especially since the sound had entered his mind, not through the thought-link, but through his ears. He stood from his seat and smiled broadly.

Mark's disembodied voice came through the link, "It's a boy."

Tom's voice shook slightly. "Is it—?"

Mark cut him off. "It's healthy, and by all appearances, normal."

"But what about its—"

"I'll check its cells as soon as I've finished with the birthing procedures. But I can tell you the answer now, if you prefer."

Half of Tom's smile faded, but half remained. "Don't bother," he said slowly. "I know the answer." Then added quickly, "But I still want you to check."

"I know; I know. I'm as eager as you to verify the obvious."

Chapter 43

Baby

After shaking Sammy's hand vigorously and slapping him on the shoulder a couple of times, Tom sat down next to Barb's bed and spoke to her softly. "How are you feeling?"

She was sitting up, cuddling the baby in her arms. "Fine," she said, smiling. "It wasn't nearly as painful as I'd expected."

"The drugs," Tom said with a nod.

"He didn't give me any."

"You're kidding." Tom frowned for a moment, but then brightened. "Must have been the nano-robots."

Barb nodded. "That was Mark's guess."

Tom smiled and looked at the baby. "So how's the little booger doing?"

"Just fine. Would you like to hold him?"

"I don't know. I . . . I might hurt him."

"Nonsense." And she proceeded to tell him the proper way to support the child's head.

Tom took the newborn in his arms. He smiled into its cute little face, bounced him slightly, and tried speaking a few simple sounds to him. "Mmmaaa-mmmmaaa," and "Daaaa-daaa." He had to say these things with his mouth, of course. The child didn't have an implanted computer yet, and even if it had one it wouldn't have had time to develop the skills needed to use it properly.

Mark entered the room looking serious.

Tom turned to face him, expectantly.

Mark looked at the baby, then nodded at Tom. "I have the results." He turned and gave Barb a gentle, reassuring smile. "Your boy is healthy and normal in every way," he said, "except that, like us, his body contains not a single organic cell."

Chapter 44

A Request Macabre

Day 43

Seven days after Barb's baby was born, Mark had accumulated enough measurements to prove that the boy's little bones were growing at a normal rate. More time would have to elapse before he could be certain the soft tissues were also growing normally. He intended to monitor the boy's progress closely, to confirm at every stage of development that the nano-robots truly understood how to grow a healthy human adult from a tiny baby boy; and to make sure that they preformed this task no faster than the usual speed.

Later that day, Doctor Williams' body was finally complete. Mark took him off sedation at noon.

An hour later—after enjoying a light lunch of steaming tomato soup—Mark found Tom walking by the lake and joined him. The two men strolled leisurely, enjoying small-talk and a few tidbits of recent town gossip. It was at this point that the old captain surprised Mark by asking him to have the commander requisition something for him. Something unusual.

Mark stopped walking and stared at Tom, clearly shocked. Tom looked back at him, but with an odd calmness. The air between them changed. Neither spoke for almost a minute. Finally Mark asked, "Are you sure you want this?"

Tom said, "Yes."

"It may not work," Mark added. "You know that, don't you? It may not work at all!"

Tom nodded; slowly, calmly. "I know."

Mark hesitated, nervously, as though looking for a better excuse. "And the military may not—"

"They'll do it," Tom interrupted with quiet confidence.

Mark tried to read Tom's mind through a detailed visual analysis of his eyes; first one, then the other. "How can you be so sure?"

"Because as soon as you make the request, they'll know the reason behind it. And while they may never admit to it, they'll want to know the answer too."

Mark looked at the ground and shook his head slowly. He wanted to feel as though this was wrong—terribly, hideously wrong. But was it? *Damn. Now I want to know if it'll work. And Tom's probably right about the military, they may blanch at the question, but they'll sure as hell fall all over themselves helping him provide them with the answer.* Mark shrugged at the ground, and said, "Okay. I'll ask her."

Tom looked up at the sky and whispered something brief, and unintelligible, through his mouth. Still looking up, he smiled, tight-lipped; then squeezed his eyes shut, forcing tears out onto his eyelashes.

Chapter 45

Hidden Secret

The commander squirmed in her command chair. Its form-fitting contours, thick padding and silky texture had become strangely uncomfortable. "I don't know, doctor; this request is highly unusual." She blinked a few times, then raised a hand to wipe her forehead. "It's one that would involve a lot of red tape: both civilian and military. I'm not saying it can't be done, mind you. Only that it would be difficult and time consuming." She hesitated a moment, trying to think.

At the request's first mention, she was only disturbed by what it implied about Captain Vickery's mental state. The old man must have decided he'll be quarantined down there for the rest of his life. Not that that's impossible—he has less than twenty years left.

But the more she thought about this request, the more convinced she was that there was something behind it. Something Mark was leaving unsaid; verbally hiding it from her. Something he was ashamed of, perhaps. She tried to guess the secret. The answer seemed to dance about in her subconscious, just out of reach.

And then it came to her.

Her eyes opened wide and a chill spread across the skin of her chest; a chill as cold as if ice water had been poured directly onto her clothing. In her shock, she almost blurted out: *Surely they don't expect! No! That's insane!*

But she knew it was not insane; not after what had transpired so far. She composed herself, and tried to pretend that her eyes had not flared and her mouth had not moved involuntarily. "Doctor, are you sure that this would be good for him? It strikes me as more than just a bit morbid."

Mark bit his tongue. She observed this in the image.

"The man is grieving," he said with a straight face. "It may be difficult for him at first, but it will help him in the long run."

The commander managed a convincing shrug. "Naturally, I defer to your judgement. You've been with him long enough to observe his mental and emotional make-up. I will begin the procedures."

Chapter 46

Cold Shipment

Day 118

The heavy digging machine rolled slowly across the hard, white snowy ground under a black star-filled sky. Its domed enclosure reflected the faint light of the distant sun and protected its driver from the near perfect vacuum on this airless world. Overall, the machine resembled a small antique military tank; except that it was painted bright green, and instead of a large gun barrel sticking out of its turret, it possessed a pair of oversized robotic arms. These arms now held high a long stainless steel box.

The digging machine entered a large door in a wide building. It paused as the airlock worked through its cycles, then rolled into a huge warehouse. The robotic arms lowered the long stainless steel box into a chrome-plated shipping crate cooled by liquid nitrogen.

A hatch flipped open on the machine's dome and a short fat man climbed out and down. "Another cold one," he said. "Ready for delivery."

A woman, even fatter than he, stepped closer. "We both lost the betting pool," she said.

"What? But I bought eight squares!"

"I know." She smiled, coyly; as though amused at his misfortune. "Eddie won."

"How many squares did he buy?"

"Same as me. Just one."

"Damn!"

"Who you got there?" she asked, nodding toward the cryonic shipping crate.

"Huh? Oh, number 11829."

"Good; there's a military transport due in two hours to pick it up."

"Military?" he asked. "Since when does the military deliver corpsicles?"

"I don't know. It's a new one on me. I already checked; she's not military."

The man frowned. "Maybe she was important, or famous."

The fat woman shrugged. "I've never heard of her."

"What was her name?"

"Maggie Vickery."

The End.

About the Author

Stephen Euin Cobb, born in South Carolina, spent the formative years from three to twenty-seven in the western suburbs of Chicago, before moving back to South Carolina.

Before realizing his dream of publishing his novel, the author earned his keep in a variety of professions, including bank teller, construction worker and long-haul truck driver.

His first love, however, has always been science. Thanks to after-school reruns of Star Trek, the televised Apollo program and numerous second-hand science fiction books—he developed a lifelong fascination with astronomy. He considers himself to have officially become an amateur astronomer at the age of thirteen; when he peered through his father's telescope and found his first planet (other than the one he'd been standing on and ignoring for so many years). Saturn looked pale and very small, but it was clearly another world. An *alien* world!

During the ensuing years Stephen has enjoyed interests in many different areas of science, such as chemistry and physics, but sees astronomy as the foundation to all other sciences, since they all exist within its huge bounds.

At the age of twenty-seven he'd grown weary of the snow and ice of Chicago winters and moved back south. He lived a hermit-like existence of writing and working until he was forty-three years old. It was at this time that he met and married the woman of his dreams: Michelle Ann Turner. He insists it was at this point that his life became complete.

They now reside where it hardly ever snows—South Carolina, with their "third family member", their dog, Baby.